OPERATOR 5:
WINGED HORDES OF THE YELLOW VULTURE

SECRET SERVICE OPERATOR #5 ™

AMERICA'S UNDERCOVER ACE

WINGED HORDES OF THE YELLOW VULTURE

By Curtis Steele

POPULAR PUBLICATIONS • 2026

PUBLISHING HISTORY

"Winged Hordes of the Yellow Vulture" originally appeared in the May/June, 1939 (Vol. 12, No. 1) issue of *Operator #5* magazine. Copyright © 2026 by Argosy Communications, Inc. All rights reserved.

CHAPTER 1
DOOMED AMERICA

JIMMY CHRISTOPHER'S alert blue eyes kindled with repressed excitement and his lithe-muscled, well poised figure seemed to gather something in stature, something in abounding vitality—as the army bombing plane, in which he was speeding westward, flew over the peaks of the Sierra Madres and dipped down toward the California coastal plain. Now Los Angeles could not be much farther—Los Angeles and *what?*

That question had been uppermost in his mind ever since the speedy bomber had taken to the air from Washington's Sheridan Field. For that matter, it had been gnawing at his thoughts ever since the tragic telephone message from George Keyes.

"I am the only one who is left, Operator 5," Jimmy remembered the quaver in the voice of the man who had, two months before, led a small undercover group into Asia. "The rest are all dead; and I am going to be with them very soon. I have been through hell—locked up in it for days—and now it is raging in my body. I'm a leper, Operator 5—victim of a virulent, incurable disease!

"Don't be shocked—you are going to become very accustomed to lepers. There are thousands of horrible cases of leprosy being propagated in China—yes, I said 'propagated.' By the Japanese government. Thousands of healthy men and women

1

who are being inoculated with the disease. Why? So that they can bring it to America—"

That was when the roar of a shot had stilled Keyes' lips—but the bullet that must have cut him down had not silenced George Keyes permanently. Jimmy had gotten in touch with his San Francisco office immediately, had set his men on Keyes' trail; but a day and a half later, before they had anything to report on him, a coded telegram signed with his service designation had arrived at Jimmy's desk.

"Still alive—but now there will not be much longer to go, thank God!" it had read. "Unable to make further report unless I can talk with you. My message urgent. Please come while there is time." And the address seemed to be that of a rooming-house—in Los Angeles!

The threatened doom that Rai Kasuga-Tosa had brought from Asia in his super-rocketships had been met and defeated—by American brains and American courage. Kasuga-Tosa and his fearsome invaders were dead, his engines of destruction consumed by their own flames. Once more America seemed to have escaped certain conquest and enslavement. But George Keyes was no man's fool; no excitable youngster who would go off half-cocked....

That alarming telephone warning, Jimmy Christopher knew, must have had a firm basis in fact. It was, of course, possible that the menace Keyes had discovered had been dissipated with the wiping out of the Kasuga-Tosa expedition—but, with so ghastly a threat as the spreading of leprosy involved, Jimmy could take no chances. Eternal vigilance must be his creed if American

independence was to be preserved; and, like a sleepless watch-dog, he was up and straining at the leash the moment there came even a hint of an alarm.

Now he was speeding to George Keyes' bedside, anxious to meet his agent before he died. But the persistent sense of uneasiness that had seized upon him when he read that telegram still gripped him. Instinctively he sensed that something about the whole setup was not as it ought to be. Keyes' half-finished telephone conversation, the shot that had cut it short, the telegram from a city nearly three hundred miles from where he had phoned—somehow these details did not jibe....

JIMMY'S NERVES were atingle as the bomber glided to a stop in the Los Angeles airport. Quickly his trained, all-observing eyes flashed around the field, at the planes that were coming and going, the passengers and spectators. And almost at once he knew that his half-sensed suspicions were well founded. He was being trailed. Not only by four of his own operatives, whom he had ordered to meet the plane but to give him no recognition. Three of those he spotted. But now there were two *other* men shadowing him; two who stepped into a car which took up his trail as soon as he hailed a cab and started off in it.

So there *were* others who knew that Operator 5 was coming to Los Angeles—sufficiently interested to await his arrival and shadow him the moment he reached the city!

But the pursuers seemed to be satisfied merely to keep him in sight. They made no attempt to cut down the distance that separated the two machines; even let it increase now that the way had led toward the outskirts of the city, into a neighborhood once fashionable but at present drifted into a backwater in which there was little traffic.

Instead of the rooming-house which he expected, Jimmy discovered that the address to which he had been directed was an elaborate old mansion. A large estate that had been transformed into a private sanitarium, he discovered when a courteous, white-uniformed attendant admitted him.

"Mr. Keyes?" The man looked doubtful. "I don't know whether he is well enough to see anybody, but if you will wait—"

Jimmy waited, and five minutes later the attendant was back, to escort him to a room on the second floor. A room with drawn blinds, lit only dimly—but sufficient to reveal the ghastly horror that lay on the bed in its center. George Keyes! Jimmy stared with popping eyes. He could see nothing but a shrunken creature with a curiously pointed, dog-like face that was half-eaten away by the frightful ravages of leprosy! A dark, gruesomely discolored face that no longer even remotely resembled the healthy, full-cheeked young countenance he knew so well!

"George…." The name came hesitantly from his suddenly dry lips. "You wanted to see me, George?" Jimmy waited.

The terrible, face-filling eyes stared at him dumbly; the nearly dead sufferer did not seem to understand.

"George…." Jimmy tried again. "This is Operator 5…."

This time his effort produced results. The sound of his name acted like magic. The big eyes rounded even more startlingly, and the ragged, withered lips began to move.

"Doomed—all of us doomed!" came from them in a croaking voice that was curiously, creepily, like the yapping of a mongrel dog. "Whole country is doomed—unless we surrender. No hope in fighting—you can't fight Japan. You can't fight leprosy—you hear?" His voice grew stronger, became tinged with hysteria, as he read the dissent in Jimmy's pitying eyes. "You can't fight—unless you want to be like me!"

Now he was screaming shrilly, and suddenly he leaped out of bed; a repulsive skeleton, no more than the fragment of a man who was in the last stages of the Asiatic plague. Like a madman, he hurled himself forward, his skinny, sore-encrusted arms stretched wide, his half-consumed fingers clutching, before Jimmy had time to leap backward and send his chair flying across the room behind him.

The horrible hands grasped his clothing—but at that moment a gun roared almost at Jimmy's back. Two shots, one a split-second after the other. The first bored a hole in the scaly forehead; the second flung the plague-ridden creature back on his heels, to drop, twitching, on the floor, a look of incredulous surprise in the agonized eyes—a third bullet drilled through the body that had already ended its misery.

DESPITE HIMSELF, Jimmy felt a surge of relief flow through him as he stepped away from the wall against which he had flung himself. Perspiration beaded his forehead and the backs of his hands—and then he turned to stare into a smiling yellow face that regarded him sardonically. A Japanese face—and yet one that was odd for a Nipponese. Slanting eyes that were close-set above a prominent, hawk-like nose; a receding chin that made the upper jaw contribute to the beak-like suggestion of the nose; these beneath an almost bald scalp—

the whole head thrust forward on hunched shoulders.

Instinctively one word flashed into Jimmy's mind—*vulture!* And he knew that he was staring into the evil eyes of Moto Taronago, the 'Yellow Vulture,' head of the Japanese secret police. The Yellow Vulture—whose diabolical cunning was credited with having done more than even the Japanese military and naval forces in bringing about the complete subjugation of Asia!

A dozen tales of this man's artful scheming, his ruthless double-crossing, his inhuman barbarity, ran through Jimmy's mind as those inscrutable eyes regarded him with mock concern.

"They should not have let you see him—a man in that condition," Taronago shook his baldish head disapprovingly. "Had he gotten his hands on your flesh his touch would have meant certain contamination. It is fortunate for you, Operator 5, that I was in time—"

"You set this stage deliberately, Taronago," Jimmy cut through his mocking pretense. "You timed that murder devilishly—but what is your game? What are you doing here in America?"

"So you know Taronago?" The Japanese half-bowed, but the Luger that he seemed to have forgotten in his hand was alert, ready for split-second action, its muzzle never swerving from Jimmy. "Then know, too, my unappreciative friend, that I am here as the advance agent of the Imperial Japanese navy, which will very soon arrive off this coast, ready to occupy its principal cities. Your man knew whereof he spoke. If you have the wisdom for which men give you credit, you will be guided by his advice—for I am also the forerunner of a pestilence that will sweep this entire continent from coast to coast!"

Blandly, with that mocking smile like a mask on his evil face, the Yellow Vulture made his outrageous admissions. But Jimmy's keen eyes had already caught the glint of guns from a doorway, from a closet across the room, from behind a white draw-curtain, from beyond the disordered bed. He was covered from every direction; would be cut down by a rain of lead at the first move he tried to make toward the taunting devil.

"You have seen your man die—mercifully," the suave voice prodded at him. "Had I allowed him to live on, his end would have been far more distressing to watch. That unpleasant sight will be witnessed in every corner of this land unless you have the wisdom to prevent it, Operator 5. Submission is the only alternative to utter desolation by the worst plague the world has ever known—submission to the sovereignty of his Imperial Highness, the Mikado."

Jimmy's fingers itched for his guns, itched to close on that yellow throat. If there was only a chance of reaching Taronago and ending the monster's evil life, he would have thrown himself forward eagerly, content to die in order to rid the world of such a menace. But blasting lead would hurl him back all too quickly; would leave America defenseless, not even aware of this plotting schemer at work within its borders.

"I see that you are not impressed," Taronago was regretful.

"You do not realize the immediacy of the doom that hangs over you—but perhaps I can convince you. Come with me and let me show you through this building."

JIMMY ACCEPTED that invitation eagerly. Now, he told himself, he might find the chance for a break—but that hope was short-lived. Those watchful guns followed him. In the apparently deserted hallway he caught the telltale gleam of light on barrels; and when he glanced at Taronago the man's cynical smile told him that he had been allowed to keep his guns only as a contemptuous gesture.

And then suddenly he forgot his helplessness in a rush of horror that overwhelmed him!

Through four floors of that long, rambling building Taronago led him, to open door after door of rooms that had become cells—barred cells tenanted by hundreds of men and women who were victims of the plague in its most advanced stages! Hundreds of white men and women who stared at him with hopeless, stricken eyes; whose insane jabbering and mad screams stabbed into his brain; whose ghastly, disease-rotted bodies filled him with horror and loathing that chilled his blood!

The building was a pesthouse, a ghastly place of the damned!

"Most unfortunate." Taronago shook his head in mock sympathy. "It is hard to believe that a few days ago these people were all well and happy. That was before they met your man Keyes. You see how swiftly this disease does its work—far more terribly than leprosy as we used to know it. Credit that to the able scientists of Japan, where, unlike in America, we say little of what our great men accomplish.

"But now we are ready that America and the rest of the world shall know what we have prepared for those who oppose us!" he lashed out savagely, the unctuous voice cast aside for that of the born dictator. "The key to this building is in your hands, Operator 5. Before you leave here you are going to advise your President Warren to make terms with me—or the doors will be thrown open and these poor wretches will be driven out into Los Angeles, to spread the plague like wildfire throughout the city!" Jimmy Christopher's skin crawled at that appalling prospect! Once these disease-maddened victims were turned loose there would be no stopping them. All of Los Angeles would be turned into a charnel-house, and after that, California—the nation, from coast to coast! What the Japanese armies could not hope to win by years of fighting, the fiendish scientists who had cultivated this fearful pestilence would accomplish in a few terrible weeks....

But the doors of that building must never be opened! These poor wretches must be put out of their hopeless misery, and the foul place must be burned over their contagion-breeding corpses. That was what he had to accomplish, Jimmy realized grimly—and his thoughts turned to his agents who had trailed him to that building. They had been instructed to give him twenty minutes; then they were to come in, with the police at their backs, if necessary.

It was more than twenty minutes since he had been admitted by the white-uniformed attendant. Twenty-five, a glance at his watch revealed. Jimmy strained his ears as Taronago led him back to the first floor. Tensely he waited for the first sound

10

that would send him into desperate action. But the main floor was quiet—and now the Yellow Vulture was leading the way to a stairs going down to the basement.

Jimmy preceded him, as the Japanese stepped back with elaborate mock courtesy; down to another floor that was only a repetition of those above—until suddenly he seemed to freeze where he stood, unable to move a muscle as he stared into one of those cell-lined rooms. There were four cells in that chamber, and in each of them was a disease-eaten leper—and one of the agents who had followed him from the airport!

The men on whose aid he had counted were even more helpless than he—were doing their best to fight off the mad creatures that swarmed over them nauseatingly!

"Just a precaution it seemed best to take so that we would not be interrupted," Moto Taronago purred—but in his moment of triumph he relaxed his vigilance, ever so slightly.

That was all that Jimmy Christopher needed. In that instant he was inside the room and Taronago was in the doorway, momentarily blocking it and shielding his captive from the watchful guns in the hallway. Apparently stunned and utterly disarmed by the predicament in which he found his men, Jimmy suddenly sprang into whirlwind action. With a diving lunge that threw him to one side, he crashed into the Jap and knocked him off-balance—and in the same moment seized his gun-wrist, just as the weapon roared and a bullet whistled by his ear.

Before Taronago could press the trigger a second time his arm was twisted half out of its socket, and he was lifted from his feet, to sail through the air and land on the floor with sickening force.

11

Too late he realized that he had fallen victim to a well known grip in the manual of his own native ju-jitsu.

Like a flash Jimmy was at the door, had slammed it shut and backed against it, his automatics in his hands and trained on the Jap, who was just scrambling to his feet.

"Open those cells, Taronago!" he snapped. "Quick—or I'll take the keys from your dead body!"

Taronago needed no further urging. He knew death when it stared him in the eye, and he had no desire to become better acquainted with it. Dropping his gun to the floor, he took out what proved to be a master-key and unlocked one barred door after the other. He released the imprisoned agents and slammed the door on the drooling lepers who tried to swarm out after them.

"Now we're going out of this door, upstairs and out of the building," Jimmy snapped. "You are walking right in front of me, Taronago—and if you think any of your killers can get me before I blow the life out of you, let him try it!"

THE MOCKING smile was gone from the vulture face by now. It had become a mask of malevolent hatred, as the Jap stepped out into the corridor with two gun muzzles pressing close against his ribs. Three crisp sentences snapped from his lips in staccato Japanese—and Jimmy, who had once made his way about freely in Japan, using only the native language, knew that he was ordering his unseen gunmen to withhold their fire.

The length of the corridor that grim procession marched, until they were almost to the stairway. Once up that, the main doorway of the building would be but a short dash; and then he would hold Taronago as hostage while his men went for aid to combat this frightful peril.

The foot of the stairs. Taronago started up onto the first step—and Jimmy tensed as a door at the side of the corridor opened and a man was framed in the doorway. A white-uniformed man who wore a surgeon's mask and rubber gloves. Wide-eyed and apparently taken by complete surprise, he gaped at them and made a half-gesture to raise his hands as one of Jimmy's guns swung to cover him.

That bit of drama took no more than a fraction of a second—but that was sufficient. It deflected Jimmy's attention just long enough for Taronago to clap one hand down on the newel-post at the foot of the stairs—and instantly the entire staircase left the floor and shot upward.

The up-swinging lower step caught Jimmy's arms and knocked them upward. His guns roared harmlessly; and then he was on the floor, was scrambling to his feet as the staircase clicked into place and filled the stairwell completely. Taronago had escaped, had been borne upward by that hinge-operated elevator; and they were trapped in the basement!

Instantly Jimmy whirled to the doorway where that white-uniformed figure had appeared so opportunely, but now the man had disappeared—and through the doorway swarmed savage-faced Japanese gunman. Jimmy's bullets met them before they had crossed the threshold, mowed down four of them. Then, barely in time, he whipped around to trigger three shots at attackers who had sprung from other places of concealment.

Now the basement was a bedlam. Wilkinson, the agent

who had picked up Taronago's Luger, was emptying it into the oncoming Japs, while the other three agents rushed forward to meet the enemy with their bare hands. Two of them went down before they could come to grips with the Japanese; the third was locked in a desperate struggle with a burly giant, grimly wresting his gun from him.

That much Jimmy saw in a desperate flash. Then he was overwhelmed, was blazing away at the on-coming Japs and then flailing at their heads with his gun barrels. He seemed to bear a charmed life in that savage mêlée. Men went down all around him. Hurling himself past their falling bodies, he was fighting clear—when a shout of alarm stopped him.

"They're letting the lepers out!" Wilkinson yelled.

Jimmy's gun became leaden things in his hands as he stared down that smoky, body-strewn corridor. Wilkinson was right. While these gunmen had been keeping him and his men busy, their devilish mates had been at work unlocking the cells. Out into the corridor swarmed the lepers, urged on by the Japanese, who herded them to the rear, where there must be another stairway—another door that would turn them loose on Los Angeles!

It was too late now to stop that stampede; too late to attempt to head it off and drive the disease-ridden creatures back into their cells. There was only one way to save the city from them—and Jimmy took it.

On the third finger of his left hand was a curiously wrought ring; a ring encrusted with a skull that bore the numeral "5" in its forehead. An ordinary appearing ring to anyone who did not know its secret—but beneath that skull lay concealed a quantity of an explosive so powerful that it would bring this entire building down in ruins.

A suicide ring, to be resorted to only in the last emergency— but when Operator 5 saw that disease-ridden horde about to be turned loose on his America, the defenseless country he loved better than life itself, he knew that the supreme emergency was at hand.

Tight-lipped and frozen-faced, he grasped the top of that ring and twisted it, plucked out the potent little capsule—and hurled it away from him just as the white-uniformed surgeon sprang from nowhere and leaped at him. This was the end... but Jimmy Christopher went down fighting. His fist lashed out at the fellow, caught him on the point of the jaw. But the surgeon's rush swept him off his feet, carried him over backward—just as the whole world seemed to dissolve in a tremendous, ear-splitting crash!

Blinding light stabbed into his eyes and added to the stunning pain of that fearful concussion. Blinding light that seemed to come from the gateway of a roaring, screaming hell that closed in on him and blotted itself out in the all-enveloping blackness that he knew must be death....

IT WAS a week later that a silent, sober-faced little group gathered in President Andrew Warren's White House study. The Chief Executive sat at his desk; sat like one stunned, his eyes filmed, his rugged face working as he fought to control his emotion.

"It hardly seems possible. I can hardly believe that Jimmy is gone... and yet I have always feared that this moment would come," he said huskily. "He should have died a hundred times over with the chances he has taken, and yet he always came through safely... until *now*...."

There were two cabinet officers in that conference, two Secret Service men, several high-ranking army and navy officers, and three of those who had always been dearest to Jimmy Christopher. Three who now sat, dry-eyed and haggard-faced, trying to avoid the President's eyes.

Well they knew the bond that had developed between the man the nation knew as Operator 5 and this staunch New Englander who had arisen to take the helm of the ship of state when America most needed him. Sterling patriots both, they had found in unselfish, untiring service to their country a friendship such as comes to few men. Andrew Warren had become a second father to Jimmy Christopher. But now....

"I understand how you feel, sir," gray-haired, gaunt old John Christopher spoke softly. "I could not believe it myself. I thought there must be some mistake when Wilkinson reported what had happened. I thought that surely my boy must have escaped!"

For four days after Jimmy Christopher had flown to California not a word had been heard from him. Then it was Herbert Wilkinson who had broken the silence. From the hospital bed to which he had been confined since he was dragged, more dead than alive, out of the blazing ruin that had almost entombed him, he had called Washington to report the death of Operator 5 and everyone who had been in the building with him. It was only by a miracle, because the explosion had blown him into a disused cellar from which he had been able to crawl to safety—that he had escaped with his life.

"We immediately assigned the best men on the coast to the case, you know that," Andrew Warren recapitulated. "And now—" he stared down at the report that lay on the desk in front of him—"I fear there is no more doubt. Operator 5 died nobly in the performance of his duty. Like Samson of old, he brought a whole building down on his head in order to trap his enemies and save his country from a plague that might have meant the and of America. It is the way he would have wanted to die," he finished softly.

"But I still do not believe it!" The words came flatly, defiantly, desperately, from a pretty, chestnut-haired young woman, who sat with her white-knuckled hands tightly clenched. "Jimmy is still alive—I *feel* it. If he were dead I would know it, I am sure of that."

Diane Elliot did not look at them. Her eyes were staring blindly, looking back through the years at that moment; were seeing again the cleancut face, the sandy-haired head, the well-knit athlete's body of the man she loved and had intended to marry; were visualizing again the innumerable dangers they had shared in the service of their country. For her, Jimmy Christopher would never be dead—nor would he be for the freckle-faced, pug-nosed, wiry young stripling who sat beside her.

To Tim Donovan—another of those faithful followers who had faced death times without number at the side of Operator 5, the man who was his leader—his friend and idol could never cease to exist.

"Me, too, Di," he said, and then his voice failed him; he could only slip his hand into Diane's and squeeze her fingers.

"But the rest of Wilkinson's report has been completely confirmed, Miss Elliot," Commander Magruder reminded gently. "We know that the Japanese fleet has arrived off the California coast as Operator 5 told Wilkinson it would."

That reminder visibly added to the weight of care that burdened down President Warren's shoulders. Barely had the United States been snatched from what had seemed to be certain doom than a fresh menace suddenly loomed to confront a staggered people. With the northeastern cities laid waste by the depredations of the late Kasuga-Tosa, and with a huge Japanese fleet now threatening the Pacific Coast ports, the situation was desperate.

More than once when disaster had seemed inevitable, Operator 5 had performed a virtual miracle that had plucked salvation out of ruin—but now there was no Operator 5 to save the day....

The realization of that grim fact was plain in the eyes of each of them as they sat there trying to read the future, trying to understand what could be the meaning of this unannounced Japanese threat and endeavoring to plan how to meet it—but at the height of their council it was the voice of Operator 5 that spoke to them! A voice from the grave, speaking words of advice he never would have uttered!

It was the undercover man who was on duty in Jimmy Christopher's office who telephoned to relay those startling words.

"I have just received a code wire—Operator 5's code and his signal," he reported excitedly. "Here it is: 'The United States is facing a menace we cannot hope to combat. If we resist, the country will be overrun by thousands of lepers who have been inoculated with a particularly virulent and fast-spreading form of the plague. Within a few weeks there will be so many millions of deaths that no city in the entire country will be habitable. I strongly advise and urge immediate surrender on whatever terms Admiral Nikatchi, of the Japanese fleet, demands. There is no other hope for America!"

Utter silence hung heavy in that study as Andrew Warren copied the last word on a sheet of paper and hung up the receiver—silence that was broken by Diane Elliot's low voice.

"Now I *know* that Jimmy isn't dead," she said with grim confidence. "Those words never came from Jimmy Christopher. They were sent by whoever is holding him—and that means he must be a helpless prisoner. I am going to the coast to find out *where!*"

"That goes for me, too, Di!" Tim Donovan's voice boomed out an echo.

CHAPTER 2
THE DOG-FACED HORDE

IT WAS after eleven o'clock at night when a specially chartered plane landed Diane and Tim Donovan in Los Angeles. Too late to do much except go to a hotel and get a good night's sleep, they had decided. But Tim's eyes were alert the moment the plane's wheels touched the field. The place was almost deserted, except for a scattering of mechanics and a few passengers who were arriving for an eleven-thirty plane, but

before they had stepped into a taxi-
cab he was fairly certain that he had
detected more than one pair of eyes
which watched them with unusual
interest.

Perhaps....

Without alarming Diane, he
tried his best to watch their back-
trail, and again his sharp eyes identified what seemed to be a
trailing car—though he admitted that it might be nothing more
than other arrivals coming into the city from the airport. Exactly
as the two men with suitcases, who entered the hotel lobby and
walked to the desk as Diane and he stepped into the elevator,
might very well be nothing more than newly arrived guests.

Perhaps he was unduly suspicious, he admitted as he said
'good-night' to Diane and entered his own room, which
adjoined hers. But Jimmy Christopher had been an excellent
teacher and Tim an apt scholar. Jimmy, he knew, would take no
chances where Diane's safety was concerned, and he intended
to take none. Instead of going to bed, he moved a chair to the
connecting door between the rooms and made himself fairly
comfortable in that.

Jimmy Christopher.... Tim's thoughts turned toward his
missing chief as he nodded in the chair and fought to keep
awake; turned back to the cold winter night, years before, when
he had crouched, hungry and shivering, in a dark hallway in New
York City. The world had looked pretty dismal to the ragged
bootblack that night—but all of that had changed when he

sprang from his concealment just in time to save an unsuspecting stranger from a criminal's bullet.

That stranger had been Jimmy Christopher, Operator 5—and from that moment a new life had begun for Tim Donovan. Taken under Jimmy's wing, a new world had opened for him. Between those two had developed a remarkable trust, devotion and admiration, a relationship that could not be fated to end now, certainly....

A lump welled up into Tim's throat at the thought—and suddenly he sat bolt upright in his chair. Had that been a sound in the next room? He was almost certain of it.... And then he heard Diane's terrified scream, heard a chair go over as she sprang out of bed!

Instantly he went into action. Leaping up from the chair, he yanked it out of the way and sprang back into the middle of the room—to charge against the door like a battering ram. Twice he launched himself against it with all his strength—and the second time the impact smashed the lock and pitched him into the dark room. Scrambling to his feet, he reached the hall doorway and found the light switch—to illuminate a scene that filled him with stark horror!

Diane, her nightgown half torn from her body, was fleeing in terror from a ghastly graveling of a creature that pursued her with maniacal desire kindling the wild eyes that blazed out of a huge head! A horrible, scabrous-looking creature that seemed a thing from hell—until Tim identified it as a grotesque Mongolian idiot whose twisted face and malformed head were half eaten away by the ravages of leprosy!

For an instant Tim was almost paralyzed by that terrible sight—and then Diane tripped and fell. Her horrified scream catapulted Tim to her side in a single bound. With fingers that flinched from the contact, he grabbed the loathsome creature by the shoulder and hurled him across the room—and then met his returning charge with an uplifted chair that came down on the hideous head and smashed to fragments upon it.

Tim was at Diane's side the moment the ghastly monstrosity toppled to the floor, was bending over her solicitously and helping her to her feet—to look up in surprise as the room suddenly seemed to be filled with policemen. Half a dozen of them, come in through the hall door that now stood open. Guns ready, they glanced around the disordered room suspiciously—and then one who wore the stripes of a sergeant spied the thing on the floor, bent over it, and drew back in quick alarm.

"A leper!" he gave quick warning to the others.

They drew back as if the plague might reach out from the unconscious creature and seize them. Then instead of backing out of the room they came toward Diane.

"She's all right now," Tim tried to dismiss them. "I got in here just in time to knock him out, thank God!"

"That's all right, but she was exposed to it," the sergeant grumbled belligerently. "That thing touched her there." He nodded to the torn nightgown Diane was holding around herself. "Can't tell, she might have caught it already. We've got to take her to a hospital and quarantine her until there's no danger. Throw something around yourself, lady," he ordered Diane. "No time to get dressed; your coat'll do. We'll take you in a cab."

"But the man didn't touch me," Diane protested. "He only caught the edge of my gown and ripped it as I ran away from him."

"Maybe so—but you're going to the hospital until we find out," the sergeant snarled. "Take that blanket from the bed and wrap her in it. That's better protection than a coat," he ordered his men.

Unceremoniously they brushed Tim aside and seized Diane, wrapped the blanket around her despite her struggles—and as he watched Tim became certain that there was something decidedly wrong there. They were too anxious to get her out of the hotel in a hurry—too careless of the contagion they pretended to believe she might spread.

The watching eyes at the airport, the trailing car, the men who arrived at the hotel just after them—one after the other those suspicious circumstances flashed into his mind. Diane's pleading protests came to him as they dragged her into the hallway—and he played his hunch. Stepping to the open window, he put two fingers into his mouth and blew three short blasts in imitation of a police whistle.

The result was instantaneous. Excited shouting broke out in the hallway, and there was a mad rush for the elevator—but before they were able to reach it with their struggling burden, Tim was ahead of them. Savagely one of the uniformed men swung a fist at Diane to quiet her—and Tim's automatic came down over his head to knock him sprawling.

Again the sound of a police whistle rang through the night—but this time it was a real one, from outside. It was answered by another. After that, Tim did not have to use his gun on Diane's captors. They dropped her and sprang into the elevator, where he glimpsed the unconscious body of the operator on the floor. After them staggered the man he had almost knocked out—and Tim flattened himself over Diane just in time to miss the hail of bullets that pelted at him as the door slammed shut and the car started toward the street.

DIANE WAS in a dressing-gown and collecting her things from her room when the police again came to her door. But this time they were genuine members of the Los Angeles force. It took only a few moments to establish that the others had been unknown masqueraders, who had wounded one of the regular men as well as the elevator operator in making their get-away.

Masqueraders in police uniforms who had been intent on kidnaping Diane—and who had been on hand ready to interfere when that hideous leper broke into her room…. Men who no doubt had brought the poor creature there and turned him loose after they had opened her door…. And men who in all probability had known that Diane and Tim were coming on from Washington and had been waiting for them at the airport….

"That means Jimmy *is* alive, Di!" Tim exulted after the officers had gone. "Now I'm *sure* of it!"

"Yes," Diane agreed soberly, "and it means also that the Japanese have their agents at work even in Washington's most closely guarded circles. After this, we won't know friend from foe."

Diane and Tim had learned enough in their talk with the police that night to convince them that Los Angeles was a town

24

on edge, a town with a bad case of incipient hysteria—and in the morning they found that they had diagnosed correctly.

"We tried our best to try to hush up the story of the explosion in the New Life Sanitarium," Mayor John Hunter told them. "Especially the leprosy angle of it. When the excavators found the first of those disease-rotted corpses we barred everyone from the scene and swore the diggers to secrecy. But the story got out in spite of that. Every newspaper had it by night, and everybody in the city knew it by the next morning."

"Of course," Diane nodded. "The story was spread deliberately. Probably by phone calls—anonymous tips—that sort of thing. The idea was to spread panic."

"It certainly succeeded," Hunter mopped his bald head. "We had a regular wave of the jitters, and it isn't over yet. The very mention of a leper is enough to create a panic. We are doing all that we can to restore public confidence, and this morning I have called a meeting of some of our leading citizens to form a defense committee."

Diane and Tim Donovan were present when that committee organized, and they studied its members keenly. There were two dozen of them, representatives of the city's professions and commercial interests. Laird Sommerville, the leading banker of Southern California; Hubert Muncaster, president of the Los Angeles Bar Association; Frank Hutchinson, publisher of the *Examiner;* Frederick Steckel, eminent physician and surgeon; Enoch Schrader, the famed super-spectacle motion picture producer; Leon Anthony, the brilliant director who was his

He swung the great light like a flail!

assistant; Ralph Baylor, the nation's reigning move star—and nearly a score of lesser lights.

From the start it was obvious that they would accomplish nothing; that Mayor Hunter's object in bringing them together was simply to capitalize on their well known names in order to restore public confidence. But one in that gathering caught Tim Donovan's attention at once—Leon Anthony. There was something about the director's face that was hauntingly familiar, and as Tim studied it he became almost certain that Anthony, with sufficient make-up to provide a disguise, had been one of those masquerading policemen who had tried to kidnap Diane!

Perhaps he was mistaken. He could not be sure—and yet half a dozen times, as the meeting progressed, he caught Anthony's eyes on Diane… caught him watching her, staring at her intently.

The meeting accomplished little—but the bombshell that Enoch Schrader exploded in the midst of it brought Diane and Tim up on the edges of their seats. It was Diane who precipitated the surprise by trying to uncover information about Jimmy, news of whose presence and death in the New Life Sanitarium explosion had been carefully guarded, even from Mayor Hunter. So far as the local authorities knew, several Secret Service men had been killed in the explosion, but their identities had remained unknown.

"Operator 5 should be here in Los Angeles at any hour," Diane hazarded, as she watched keenly the faces of her listeners. "I am sure that he will welcome the aid of your committee. Until he arrives, Mr. Donovan and I, who are his assistants, will do anything—"

"But—but Operator 5 *is* here!" Enoch Schrader exclaimed in wide-eyed bewilderment. "That is—that is, I understood he wanted to keep his presence here unknown," he stammered embarrassedly.

Diane smiled encouragement, nodded, and Schrader seemed to take confidence, to feel that his lips were unsealed.

"I have been collaborating with him in the filming of what will be an outstanding picture, one which will dramatize for the rest of the nation the danger of a Japanese invasion that we face here in California. A super-spectacle, if I may be permitted to say so, which will sound a clarion call to American patriotism and rouse our people from the false security that encompasses them and imperils our independence."

It was Mayor Hunter who interrupted that oratorical flight. "Where can Operator 5 be located, Mr. Schrader? Can you tell us that?"

Again the producer looked embarrassed. "I don't know that myself. I rather understood Operator 5 wanted nobody to know it," he looked significantly at Diane. "But we have hired and uniformed thousands of extras, and most of the invasion scenes will be shot today. In all probability I will see him then."

That was all Diane and Tim needed to know. As soon as the meeting adjourned, they hurried out of the City Hall and hired a taxi to take them to Hollywood. They debated this amazing development.

"I can't understand it," Diane puzzled again and again. "It isn't like Jimmy to keep us in the darkness this way. He must know that we have heard he is dead—and he knows how the news of his death would affect all of us. It isn't like him to let us go on believing that. And if he is alive and at work here in Hollywood, then that telegram was genuine—and that *couldn't* have been from Jimmy!"

For long minutes, as the taxi sped out along Hollywood Boulevard, Tim was silent, deep in meditation; but at last he reached a decision.

"I don't know." He shook his head. "But, whatever it is, Jimmy has a reason for what he is doing, and a mighty good one, too—you can depend on that." And with that profession of faith he was content....

THEIR ARRIVAL at the huge Schrader studio, with its throngs of employees and extras coming and going, put an end to their pondering. Tim helped Diana out and turned to pay the driver—but suddenly she grasped his arm. Instantly he saw what had caught her attention—and together they stared in blank amazement at a figure they would have recognized anywhere.

Jimmy Christopher! They saw him for only a few moments, as he hurried surreptitiously from a small private entrance and almost ran to where a car waited for him at the curb—but there could be no mistaking him. No mistaking that figure or the glimpse they had caught of his face....

"Jimmy!" came softly, incredulously from Diane's lips. "It was Jimmy—but it *couldn't* be, Tim! I feel like a person in a nightmare, seeing people who aren't real—"

"He was real, all right," Tim said grimly. "You're right, Di—I'd have sworn that was Jimmy, but it couldn't have been. That means there is something mighty rotten going on—and it's up to us to find out what it is. I'm going to follow that car," he decided quickly. "You stay here and take care of this end, Di. That fellow must have some reason for filming this invasion picture."

Before she could agree or protest, he had stepped back into the cab, clipped an order to the driver, and was off on the trail of the car that was just disappearing in the direction of Sunset Boulevard.

Jimmy Christopher there in Hollywood…. A fake Jimmy Christopher taking his place…. Either one or the other of them filming what sounded like a sensible propaganda picture…. The more Diane thought about it, the less sense it all made; and when she stepped into that land of make-believe that was the Schrader studio she felt like one of the strange and outlandishly garbed characters who surrounded her on every side.

The huge studio, with its dozens of sound stages and acres of fantastic sets, seemed like a bewildering maze; but at last she found the amazingly realistic reproduction of Los Angeles' principal streets which was the set for the Japanese invasion scene. Some of the smaller invasion scenes had already been filmed, but now Leon Anthony was on hand, and preparations for the mass invasion were being completed.

Out of what appeared to be inextricable confusion, Anthony's megaphoned directions quickly brought order. The Los Angeles set was cleared of all but the performers. Pedestrians began to take their places on its sidewalks, taxis idled at the curbs or waited for the signal to start moving along the streets—and off to one side an army of more than a thousand Japanese soldiers stood resting on their guns.

31

Everything was in readiness. From his high perch Leon Anthony surveyed the scene and raised his whistle to his lips— but before he could blow it wild consternation seemed to strike the pseudo-Japanese. Yells of terror went up from among them, and then blind panic seized the whole "army." Pell-mell they dashed across the set.

"Hold everything!" Anthony bellowed wildly, and blew on his whistle until he was red in the face.

But the terrified extras paid no attention to him. Flinging away their guns, they ran in a wild rout. After them came another army; an army of ghastly-looking Chinamen, their clothing filthy rags, their faces and bodies gnawed and eaten away by the fearful ravages of leprosy!

"Lepers!" the terrified howl went up from hundreds of throats, and the rout became a blind, panic-stricken stampede.

Lepers—there were hundreds of them! Poor creatures who looked more like animals than men and women. Their faces deformed and dog-snouted, their bodies bent, hunched over, with arms dangling loosely as they scuttled everywhere—they were a frightful, shocking sight. Whining and yapping like a pack of mad dogs, they flung themselves upon the extras, upon the camera-men, the electricians everyone within reach.

In little more than a minute their advent had desolated the Los Angeles set. But that did not stop them. As she fled with the others, Diane saw that the lepers were spreading everywhere on the huge movie lot—were invading one sound stage after the other, yanking open doors of dressing-rooms and swarm-

ing into them—pursuing the terrified performers and extras wherever
they fled.

Horror clutched at Diane's
throat as she watched that appalling scene—watched well known
male stars desperately trying to
hold off the obscene creatures who
swarmed over them; watched beau-
tiful actresses pursued and clutched

in the arms of those nauseous death-carriers. A wild riot in
which there seemed to be no way of escape. Wherever the terrified victims turned, the lepers were there in swarms to cut them
off—and then Diane realized that there must have been more
than the swarm she had seen invade the Los Angeles set. There
must have been other hundreds secreted at strategical points
throughout the lot, to be liberated to close the trap on the fleeing victims!

A ghastly maelstrom of terror-stricken people! Like a huge
masked ball that had suddenly been invaded by death, that
ghastly scene was fascinating. Japanese soldiers fought with
chorus girls, American Indians struggled with South African
natives. New York gangsters brushed Elizabethan Englishmen
out of their path—and over them all swarmed the plague-ridden Chinese! Over them all settled the clammy grip of horrible death!

Desperately men tried to fight the lepers, to beat them off
with clubs and guns—but death meant nothing to them. Only

one thought seemed to be ingrained in their brains—to spread contagion everywhere.

Panting and unable to run any further, Diane took refuge in a corner of one of the sets where she was partially hidden. From that retreat she watched the pandemonium rage, watched the terrified thousands sweep past her in a mad rush for the gates. NOW THE main rush was over; only the stragglers still went past, but even these the voracious lepers hunted down implacably. Man after man sped past with a veritable dog pack at his heels. And then a giant of a fellow came running straight in Diane's direction, with six of the pursuers yapping on his trail. Gorilla Cagle, ex-wrestler and film strongman, she recognized him—and then he tripped and was down, not twenty feet from her!

Like a hungry wolf pack they closed in on him. But before he could scramble to his feet Diane was standing over him, her automatic out of her handbag and blasting death at those slavering near-beasts. Four of them went down from deadly accurate bullets, and a fifth tripped and fell over his fellows. Not until then did the survivor hesitate and try to swerve out of the way. But by that time Cagle was on his feet.

"Seven feet of man—and went down like a kid!" he growled; and then, with a wild bellow he reached out and hammered his fist into the belly of the last of his attackers—drove in such a pile-driving blow that the leper was lifted off his feet and flung bodily into the faces of three others who came running to join him.

That much Diane saw, and then suddenly she was seized

from behind, dragged away. Desperately she tried to break loose, tried to strike out with her automatic. But her wrist was gripped and held tight… and then she saw that her captor was Leon Anthony.

The man's face was transformed, a battleground of conflicting emotions, but his lips were tightly clenched and he stared into her face with eyes that gleamed fanatically. With one arm around her waist and the other hand holding her wrist in a grip of steel, he lifted her from the ground and started to drag her toward a sound stage.

That was when Gorilla Cagle turned around and saw what was happening. With a roar like that of a mad bull, he came charging after them, to tear her from Anthony's grip as if she were a doll. Gently he put her to one side and turned to where the raging director was tearing at him—to flatten the man with one terrible bone-crushing blow of his mighty fist.

"Seven feet of man—and he thought he could stop me!" he scoffed.

That brief divertissement had given the lepers a chance to close in. A score of them came swarming toward those two isolated victims, intent on overwhelming them. But now Gorilla Cagle's fighting blood was fully aroused. His big face twisted in a savage grin as he leaped to the side of a set and seized a big Klieg light. With one tug he tore it free, grabbed it near its base and swung it around his head like a flail.

One crash smashed its lens, and after that the twisted light had jagged glass teeth which ripped and tore as he crashed it down to the right and left, battering those noisome creatures out of his way and treading them underfoot. Straight through them he carved a path for Diane; led her safely to the protection of a portable dressing-room and thrust her inside, to take his stance at the door.

The bloody havoc he created was too much even for those frenzied lepers. One by one, they went down or slunk away, and in a few minutes he had the field to himself, a primeval giant leaning on his crimsoned battle-ax, surrounded by the bloody corpses of his enemies!

There he stood on guard when Leon Anthony came dragging himself to the foot of the steps. Cagle glowered down at the broken man suspiciously, but Diane could see that the director was mortally wounded. The blow Cagle had given him, followed by a mauling by the lepers, had been too much for his frail physique. Blood was gushing from his mouth, and his face was deathly white. Quickly she came out and knelt beside him.

"Thanks," he could barely whisper. "You didn't understand—I was trying to save you. I had to save you—I knew all this last night. You are too lovely to die—too lovely to become a hideous leper. When I saw you again at the meeting this morning, I made up my mind—I had to save you. I couldn't go through with it… no matter what…."

Beyond that, Diane was never to know what he had intended to say. The crimson tide gurgled in his throat and drowned the half-voiced confession of the man who was too much a lover of beauty to be a villain. With a half-smile on his face, as if he welcomed what was coming, Leon Anthony died….

Diane rose from beside the still body and looked out over

the desolated movie lot. Where a few minutes ago thousands of people had been struggling frantically, there was now silence—the silence of death and desolation. A shiver coursed down her spine as the shuddering thought flashed into her mind that this might be symbolical of what would take place all over America in the next few weeks!

Her strong-man champion had saved her from the fate that had overtaken so many others—but the lepers had followed their terrified victims out of the studio grounds, out into Hollywood, and then on to Los Angeles. The great city was doomed.

CHAPTER 3
CITY OF HORROR

"**F**OLLOW THAT black car—but be careful you don't get too close," Tim Donovan had warned the taxi driver, as he stepped into the car in front of the Schrader studio and shut off Diane's possible objections by closing the door before she could even voice them.

He had been quite emphatic in assuring Diane that the man they had seen could not possibly have been Jimmy Christopher—but now he wondered. By every way of reasoning, he could not have been Jimmy—and yet it gave him a strange feeling to have actually looked at that well loved face and then denied its identity.

Queer, disquieting emotions surged through him as he sat in that cab and watched the rear of the car ahead of them; the car that contained—whom? If the passenger *was* Jimmy, perhaps it was a mistake to shadow him this way? No, it *couldn't* be Jimmy, he came back resolutely to his decision.

Then *who?*

Along Sunset Boulevard to Vine Street, and then east into the foothills that overlooked Hollywood, the trail led. As they turned into Appian Way, Tim's wonder grew. This was a section of luxurious homes, motion picture millionaires, mansions—and at one of the finest of them the black car swung into the driveway and disappeared.

The place was a regular palace, situated on a hilltop that overlooked the film town and commanded a view all the way to the waters of the Pacific. Thrusting a bill into the driver's hand, Tim dropped off as the cab passed the driveway. He was in time to catch a glimpse of the man he would have sworn was Jimmy Christopher, leaving the open garage and walking toward the mansion—*alone.*

So there was no chauffeur. That simplified matters. Emboldened by that knowledge, Tim skirted his way along the edge of the driveway to the rear. He found, to his satisfaction, that the house would be easy to enter. Porches and terraces were on all three floors. Quickly he spotted an open porch on the first floor, from which he would have no difficulty climbing the ornate stone pillar to a terrace directly above it.

Carefully he reconnoitered the place, but there seemed to be no signs of life; no servants in evidence. That second-floor terrace, he decided, would be his best bet—and swiftly put his plan into execution. Without mishap he reached the porch,

JIMMY CHRISTOPHER

climbed onto its railing, got a toehold in the back pillar, and in two steps was able to reach the floor of the terrace.

Again, nobody appeared when he drew himself up and cautiously stepped to the French window—to peer into a bedroom that had the unused appearance of a guest room. Noiselessly he opened the screen door and tried the knob behind it. That, too, opened readily. Slowly he pushed it back and stepped inside—and then froze where he stood as the voice of Jimmy Christopher came to his ears!

Jimmy—that *was* he! There could be no mistaking that voice! In that moment Tim cringed, like an eavesdropper caught in the act. He was almost on the point of turning back and stealing away before he should be discovered and have to face Jimmy's accusing eyes—but the strange words that impinged on his consciousness stopped him. Words that were being spoken into a telephone....

"Everything is in readiness and there can be no slip-up," he heard. "Yes, yes, I know, Taronago—there was a slip-up last night. But if I had been handling that matter for you, the girl would now be in your hands—or wherever you want her to be. You ought to know by this time—" with a low, mocking chuckle—"that Operator 5 makes no mistakes!"

That chuckle was a miscue. It jarred on Tim's nerves and sounded a warning in his brain; held him tense, listening.

"Yes...yes...everything is ready," came that so familiar voice. "I was just there and saw to the last-minute preparations. This time we are not leaving it to Anthony to do the directing. The moment the signal is given all hell will break loose."

Leon Anthony! For one horrible moment Tim had been almost fooled again by that voice, almost convinced that something unthinkably terrible had happened to Jimmy's brain—but now he knew! Now the last cobweb of uncertainty was swept from his mind, and he knew that he was listening to a diabolically clever *masquerader!* Leon Anthony *had* been one of the bogus policemen the night before, and this fellow was one of his confederates. Both of them were taking their orders from a Jap named Taronago.

Tim's pulses leaped with excitement. This masquerader knew where the real Jimmy was—or if he did not know that, he could be forced to lead the way to this Taronago, who would know! CAREFULLY TIM edged his way out into the hallway. The telephone conversation was still going on, but now it was chiefly monosyllabic from that end; the masquerader was listening, being told what to do. The voice came from a room at the other end of the corridor, Tim discovered, as he catfooted toward it. This fellow's private room, undoubtedly; and perhaps in there would be the very information that would reveal Jimmy's whereabouts. Certainly that was the first bet to copper.

By this time the telephone clicked back into its cradle Tim was in a linen closet next to the room he wanted to enter. Tensely he waited there, until he heard the telephoner leave, heard him go downstairs.

Now the way was clear! Stepping from his closet, Tim tiptoed into the room and found, as he expected, that it was a private living-room, with a bedroom adjoining. There was a desk and a large center table with a drawer filled with papers; a pad and several notebooks lying on its top. Those first—but they yielded nothing of interest; chiefly cabalistic notes and tables. Then the big table drawer.

Tim drew it open noiselessly, began to sort through the array of documents and letters, when suddenly his flesh goose-pimpled. That was a noise—somewhere at his back! Without moving, he raised his eyes to a mirror on the wall in front of him—and saw that devil, who was so remarkably like Jimmy Christopher, standing in a doorway behind him, an automatic trained squarely on his back!

"Stand just where you are!" came from the lips that should have been Jimmy's. A cold, deadly smile was on the fellow's face as he came forward and ran his fingers over Tim's hips and shoulders, to lift his automatic from its holster. "That's better," he clipped. "Now you can relax—and we can do a bit of talking. First of all, who are you?"

Tim Donovan turned around to face his captor, and stared into a face so similar to Jimmy Christopher's that the resemblance amazed—and then appalled him. Trading on this unholy duplication of Jimmy's features, this fellow could accomplish no end of harm. Passing himself off as Operator 5, he could trick almost anyone into his deviltry!

Somehow, Tim had to get the upper hand. Somehow, he had to capture this fellow—but *how?* Quickly he mapped desperate strategy.

"Tim Donovan," he answered the fellow's question—and then stared at the gun muzzle as if he expected it to spout flame and lethal lead at any moment.

42

"Tim Donovan?" the pretender repeated, and his eyebrows lifted appreciatively. "So that's why you are here—you are supposed to be a very good friend of mine, aren't you, Tim?"

"Of Jimmy's—not of yours," Tim snapped.

"Oh, so I don't quite convince you that I am Jimmy Christopher," his captor came closer. "That's interesting. You know we don't want to leave any doubt in people's minds. Suppose you tell me where I fall short."

"Yes, I'll tell you," Tim said, as he backed away from that menacing gun muzzle. "It isn't your face—that's perfect. It's your hands. Jimmy always wears a ring—like this."

He tugged at the skull-topped ring on his left hand that was a replica of Operator 5's own. But his trembling fingers could not get it off. Curiously the masquerader came closer, bent forward—and suddenly that trembling youngster came to startling life. Before the bogus Operator 5 had time to realize what was happening, his gun-wrist was imprisoned. Desperately he triggered the weapon before it dropped from his paralyzed fingers, but the bullet smashed harmlessly through a window. Then his arm was twisted painfully, almost yanked from its socket, was whipped over the young fellow's shoulder—and he went sailing across the room, to land in a heap on the floor.

"That's one way in which you fall short of Jimmy Christopher," Tim snapped, as he groped for the fallen gun that had rolled under a couch. "You are supposed to know ju-jitsu—and you ought to remember that you taught me that trick."

The gun eluded his fingers, pushed farther under the low couch; and now there was an alarming commotion downstairs.

The house had suddenly come to life. Men were shouting; feet came pounding up the stairs. There was no more time to be lost. Springing to his feet, Tim ran into the corridor and down its length to the room by which he had entered the house.

Bullets spat around his head as he reached the terrace and leaped to the ground. They buzzed after him like hornets as he ran to the garage, praying fervently that the keys would be in the car the masquerader had driven in a short while before.

They were! Flinging himself into the seat, Tim pressed the starter, threw the car into reverse and crouched low as he backed out and turned to race down the drive. Three men tried desperately to stop him, but their lead spattered harmlessly against the side of the car—and then he was clear, was headed back to Los Angeles.

THE TRIP to the heart of the city seemed endless, even though he drove at top speed; but Tim did not dare trust the police. Straight to an inconspicuous office building on Sixth Street he drove and pounded up to the unlabeled office on the second floor that was Secret Service headquarters. Four of Operator 5's men were there to greet him—and to grab for their hats the moment they heard his news.

"That is Enoch Schrader's place!" Mel Hallett, in charge of the Los Angeles office, identified the Appian Way mansion as soon as Tim described it. "So he's mixed up with the Japs, eh? Well, you've done a good job, Tim—even though this rat who calls himself Operator 5 probably will be gone by the time we get there. Brother Schrader will have a tall lot of explaining to do when we interview him."

Tim found little consolation in that. Bitterly he berated himself as he drove back to Hollywood at reckless speed. He had had the man needed to locate Jimmy Christopher right in his hands—but had let him escape. Now the fellow would be gone, and Enoch Schrader probably would have been warned to flee, as well....

The big house looked quiet and peaceful in the noon-day sun, as Tim jammed on the brakes at its curb. With two of the operatives he started for the front door, while Melvin and another ran through the drive to the rear, Tim started the assault by pounding on the door with a gun he had picked up at headquarters. At the same time his companions smashed their way through two lower windows—just as the door opened and Jimmy Christopher, gun in hand, stood on the threshold!

Tim Donovan's gun came up grimly—and then his eyes popped and his jaw dropped. The whole world seemed topsy-turvy in that moment, but this was Jimmy who was grinning at him! He was paler and thinner than the masquerader, Tim noticed, and he certainly needed a shave—but there was that indefinable something about him that none but Jimmy Christopher would ever possess no matter how much others might resemble him....

"Nice of you fellows to come to get me out of here," Jimmy

grinned, as they crowded around him with drawn guns. "But I'll go along peacefully; you won't have to drag me!"

Tim found his voice. "*Jimmy!* Then I guess you don't know anything about this bird who has been posing as you?" He quickly explained what had happened here a little while before.

"So *that* was the meaning of that shot upstairs!" Operator 5 whistled softly as he wrung Tim's hand. "You gave me the break I have been looking for ever since they brought me here and locked me up in the basement. One of the gang had just brought in my lunch when he heard that shot and turned around to listen—and I was on his neck before he could move. I knocked him out and got his gun and then shot it out with another of the guards. There were two more who had me cornered down there, but after a while they seemed to become discouraged and left. I see, now, it was because they were afraid you would be back with help, Tim.

"How did I get here?" he answered the questions they pumped at him. "You know about as much as I do. I remember blowing up the sanitarium—and then I was stretched out downstairs here in the basement. It seems I lay there a very long while, and a white-uniformed surgeon seemed to be hovering over me. Maybe so. He may have been the same one I was tangled with when the sanitarium came down on our heads. Perhaps he pulled me out of the wreckage by some exit he knew about. All that I know is that I was down there in the basement when I came to my senses."

His captors had given Operator 5 no opportunity to learn

their identity, but when he heard Tim's story he quickly put two and two together.

"Taronago is our man, of course," he outlined rapidly, "but Enoch Schrader appears to be his right-hand man. Undoubtedly the fellow you saw, Tim, was one of Schrader's actors who is an excellent impersonator. Leon Anthony, his director, you say is in it, too—and Diane is down there in the studio. They may have jumped her already! We're going there—*fast!*"

THEY DROVE fast—but not fast enough. By the time they reached Sunset Boulevard, Hollywood's main street was a place of wild terror. Screaming, panic-stricken men and women were fleeing in every direction, and on their heels came the leper horde. The horror that was to shock the entire nation had already swept the Schrader studio and was spreading out over the countryside.

Every available means of transportation had been seized by the frantic refugees—anything with which they could get away from Hollywood… and carry the pestilence with them. The appearance of Tim's automobile was the signal for a concerted rush toward it, but Operator 5 steeled himself to necessity and ordered his men to beat off the clutching hands. Into the studio, now a deserted and wreckage-strewn battleground, Tim drove; up and down avenue after avenue—until suddenly he let out an exultant whoop.

He had spied Diane and Gorilla Cagle!

"Back to Los Angeles as fast as you can make it, Tim," Jimmy Christopher ordered, as soon as the rescued pair were in the car.

"Our job now is to fight this plague before it sweeps all over Los Angeles."

Past hundreds of running, walking, hopelessly trudging fugitives they sped; hundreds of desperate souls blindly fleeing from one place of horror to a worse one—for by the time they reached Los Angeles the plague had already gripped the city. Wild panic was everywhere; fear-maddened fugitives desperately trying to fight their way into buildings to escape the prowling lepers, and being just as desperately resisted by those inside.

Jimmy's great heart ached as he passed miles of such scenes and saw a mammoth city transformed into a metropolis of misery and horror. That was what had been done to Los Angeles in not more than an hour. How much longer would it be, he asked himself, before these terrible scenes were repeated in every city and town from the Pacific to the Atlantic?

At the City Hall, Mayor Hunter and his assistants greeted Operator 5 with open arms and blanched faces.

"They are turning our city into a morgue, Operator 5!" John Hunter gasped, as tears wet his cheeks. "It's frightful—the things I have seen and the news we have heard. We tried to fight it—but the lepers seem to be all over; and I can't blame the police for thinking of themselves and their families."

"What surprises me is how swiftly the plague spread from Hollywood," Jimmy puzzled. "The outbreak here seemed almost simultaneous."

"It was," Hunter nodded his head glumly. "Some of it came from Hollywood, of course, but there were hundreds, perhaps thousands, of these diseased creatures hidden away here in the city, ready to be turned loose at the same moment. We have captured several of them—and found doctors courageous enough to work over them. This isn't only leprosy we are fighting, Operator 5. These poor leper devils have been infected with another disease as well; something that makes them rabid, like hydrophobia. That is why they attack everyone in sight."

A horde of rabid lepers let loose on defenseless America! The appalling prospect clutched at Operator 5's heart and chilled his blood. Then his fighting spirit reasserted itself and threw off the pall of horror that threatened to enervate him. Still weak from his narrow escape from death and his days of captivity, he rose to the emergency and took charge where all those around him were panic-stricken wholly and demoralized by terror.

Establishing his headquarters in City Hall, Jimmy issued crisp, assured orders that had a double effect; they accomplished results and they instilled confidence in those to whom they were addressed. Gathering around him the heads of the city departments, he mapped swift plans for arresting the spread of the plague. And, as they listened, those men who had been ready to give up and flee for their lives took new hope and buckled down to the task of fighting.

"I want every road leading into this city blockaded," he directed the police commissioner. "Nobody is to enter or to leave. Post squad-cars and machine-guns on the main highways, and a cordon of police on the others—and shoot to kill. You will be saving thousands of lives with every leper you prevent from escaping.

"Next—" he addressed them all—"I want every available

49

man—every man who is not already infected—mobilized to help carry out a huge concentration and isolation program. The western half of this city must be evacuated and turned over to the lepers. They must be forced to go there—and kept there."

THOSE ORDERS produced results. Los Angeles became an isolated city, cut off from physical contact with the rest of the world—and by the next day Operator 5 could draw his first relieved breath. At least the plague seemed to be confined within the metropolitan area. From beyond that there were no reports of outbreaks.

But within that area the spread of the disease was appalling. The number of new cases mounted so swiftly that it was apparent that the unaffected would soon be outnumbered by the stricken ones—and would be helpless to keep them under control.

Death was everywhere!

"They will break out of the western end and run riot," Mayor Hunter worried, as the leper toll mounted. "We can shoot some of them down—but they will overwhelm us before we can hope to stop them."

But Operator 5 had an answer for that. "They may be lepers—but they are Americans, also," he reminded. "I will talk to them."

From Los Angeles' combined radio network his appeal went out to them; went out to fellow-Americans, challenging them, pleading with them to save their country—and an hour after he was finished his telephone rang to inform him that a leper committee wanted to see him at the boundary.

There were a dozen of them, drawn up on their own side of

the barbed-wire barricade, when he arrived; a dozen stern-faced men who had been leaders in the industrial and social life of the city. Laird Sommerville, the banker, was their spokesman.

"We will take charge of this half of the city, Operator 5," he promised. "We will see that nobody leaves. We are already organizing companies and patrols to do our own policing. All that we ask is a supply of arms to enforce our orders."

Jimmy Christopher's eyes were moist as he turned away from that conference. Those men would keep their word, he knew. And they did. But, despite their vigilance, disease-ridden desperadoes managed to run their gauntlet—through back alleys and sewers, by ganging together and overwhelming the guards at one point on the line before it could be reinforced. Sufficient of them got through to spread contagion—and by the end of the third day it was apparent that all of Los Angeles was doomed. The only hope was to evacuate the city entirely.

That was the day that Mayor John Hunter was stricken and silently stepped across the barricade into the realm of the damned.

"I want every physician mobilized," Jimmy directed the health commissioner. "We will set up stations where all the unaffected can be examined and then passed through the police cordon into the hills."

That program went into effect immediately, but the Japanese lost no time in revealing that they were well informed of what went on in the doomed city. The evacuation order proved to be the spur that sent the Nipponese fleet into action. Closing in on San Pedro, they soon silenced its forts and naval base—and then the shells began to drop in Los Angeles.

"Get the women and children out first," Jimmy ordered; and he went on the air with an appeal for volunteers to dig trenches and erect barricades to defend the city to the last.

Thousands flocked to answer that plea, but most of them Operator 5 turned away and assigned to duty guarding the women.

"I do not want an army," he told them. "I want five thousand men at the most—a suicide battalion of men who are willing to die here in the ruins of their city in order to hold back the Japanese as long as possible. The governor is coming to our aid with militia. They are erecting an impregnable line ten miles beyond the city limits—but they need time to complete their work, and it's up to us to give it to them. If we die here we may be able to save America from the double peril of plague and invasion."

After that, his hardest task was to keep his battalion within the five-thousand limit he had set. One delegation that insisted upon being included in it was made up of film actors from the Schrader studios. Among them was Gorilla Cagle and Ralph Baylor.

"We feel that Enoch Schrader's treachery has disgraced all of us," Baylor spoke for them. "The least we can do to let the rest of the country knew where we stand is to do our part to stop the Japanese from going any farther. We're here to stay with you to the end, Operator 5."

And, from behind him, Gorilla Cagle nodded his approval.

"Seven feet of man—guess I ought to be able to hold back a few of these Jap runts!" he grinned.

Shells were landing in the stricken city with devastating regularity by the evening of the fourth day; but by then the evacuation had been completed. All who remained were the suicide volunteers who labored valiantly erecting barricades of every description—only they and the lepers....

It was eleven-thirty that night when Operator 5 sat in his City Hall headquarters with a group of assistants clustered around the spot of light that illuminated his flat-topped desk. Carefully he went over the last-minute details, for word had reached them that the Japanese had landed at San Pedro and were coming on in the morning.

"We should be able to hold out for forty-eight hours—until the city is reduced to absolute ruins," he finished. "We'll fight them every foot of the way—"

"No, you won't," a voice from the darkness knifed in and cut him short. "You're getting out of here tonight—right now. Don't make a move for a gun, any of you—we have you covered! All right, men, go in and grab them."

Out of the darkness stepped a dozen lepers, and then fifty more came pounding up the stairs from below. Jimmy backed away from his table—and saw that the street below was filled with them. The lepers had broken loose and overwhelmed their own police. No—the leper guards had gone back on their word; there in the front rank were Sommerville and Mayor John Hunter!

JIMMY TRIED hard to protect, to shame and rally them,

but they paid no attention to his words. They advanced on him warily and seized him and the others with rubber-gloved hands—dragged them out into the street and took them in cars to the Union Pacific Station, where the downcast suicide volunteers were being herded into trains and run out of town. Trains with leper crews in the engine cabs, Jimmy noted with sinking heart; trains that would keep on running north until they were hundreds of miles from Los Angeles—and the way was open for the Japanese invaders!

What Mayor Hunter had feared had come to pass—and now he was a party to it himself. The lepers had gotten completely out of control. Driven half-mad by their affliction, they were fleeing from death that would soon claim them anyway—and were delivering their countrymen into the hands of the enemy....

Most of the overpowered defenders had already been shipped away before Operator 5 and his staff arrived. They were put on the last train—but as it pulled out of the station he vowed grimly that he would be back. These panic-stricken doomed men must not be allowed to doom all America!

As soon as the train got under way he called his men together and began to make plans for overwhelming the engine crew, but that was a very difficult matter. They had been disarmed before being put aboard, and the lepers were constantly on guard. To make an abortive attempt to jump them would only increase their vigilance. Jimmy had to be sure—and yet the hours were speeding past.

It was not until after four o'clock that the opportunity came when the train stopped to take on water. The moment it began

to slow, scores of the volunteers dropped from windows and platforms—to creep up on the engine crew from the darkness and leap upon them before they could use their weapons. With the lepers tied up and isolated in one of the cars, Operator 5 took charge of the engine and began to back toward Los Angeles.

He did his best to make speed, but the back trip was necessarily slower than when the engine led the way. It was after nine the next morning before they rolled back into the city—and before they reached it they could hear terrific explosions.

"Sounds like shells," Tim Donovan said in surprise. "Guess the Japs don't know the way is wide open for them."

But Operator 5's battle-tuned ears were more sensitive.

"Not shells," he corrected grimly. "Those are ground explosions, bombings. They are blowing the city to pieces."

Los Angeles was being blown to pieces—but not by the Japanese! Jimmy Christopher's eyes widened in astonishment, and he brought the train to a halt, to disembark his men before they backed into the station. In the distance he saw the columns of Japanese marines and sailors coming on; coming on apparently unopposed—until the great Pacific Electric Terminal was blown to atoms and buried hundreds of them in the wreckage!

A city without defenders—and yet it was taking a deadly toll from the invaders. The tall *Examiner* Building suddenly bellied outward in every direction and crashed to the Japanese-crowded street. Robinson's great department store smashed down on a block-long procession of the yellow men. Broadway became a great canyon of tumbling buildings.

"The lepers!" The words came with almost sacred reverence from Jimmy's lips. "They are dying by the thousands—but they are making the Japs pay dearly for every foot of ground they take!"

As the words left his lips, Mayor Hunter came sweeping around a corner into Sixth Street at the head of thousands of the diseased men. In a moment they were locked in a fierce straggle with the invaders—only to be buried under tons of debris when the buildings on both sides of the street came tumbling down in blasted ruins!

A lump rose in Operator 5's throat as he witnessed that glorious sacrifice. He had misjudged those men—terribly. But now he bestowed on them the accolade for pure, undaunted courage.

"Let's go back to the train, men," he turned to his followers. "They wanted it that way—and God knows they have earned the right to give the orders today." Reverently he bowed to the will of the leper martyrs and left them to the graves they were making for themselves and their enemies in that city of death....

CHAPTER 4
THE DARKNESS
THAT CAME AT NOON

THE SUN had been shining brightly all morning at the R-in-a-Box ranch, but Mary Reid had been so busy that she had hardly had time to notice it. With her in the ranch-house kitchen were her daughter Luella and eight other women, the wives and daughters of their South Dakota neighbors. There was plenty of work for all of them. The huge-topped stove was covered with pots, the oven was crammed with cake and pie tins, and there was still a great deal more food being prepared—for this was circuit-court day in Tyndall, the country seat.

Court day meant a cessation of labor for the men, but plenty of it for the women. While the men-folk rode into town to renew acquaintances and hear the cases, the women of the neighborhood gathered at the R-in-a-Box to prepare for the dinner and dance that would be held there in the evening. It had been that way for years, and Mary Reid loved it.

Her eyes twinkled as they passed from one to the other of the five middle-aged friends with whom she had grown up, and then rested appreciatively on their daughters and on her own newly married Luella—already an expert ranch wife. It was days like this, she told herself contentedly, that made one realize how good it was to be alive....

"Looks like it's clouding up—and it started out to be such a fine day," Hattie Sanderson's voice broke in on her medita-

The men marches by like automatons, sleepwalkers.

tion. "Queer, too, Lon was saying only this morning he 'lowed it would be a week or more 'fore we got a drop."

Rain? The thought vaguely disturbed Mary Reid, and she walked to the door and looked toward the north, where the sky was darkening ominously. Then she stepped outside and sniffed the air, held her moistened finger up into the slight breeze—that was blowing *toward* the north.

That was strange—for the darkness was certainly coming due south, and at a swift pace, too.... An anxious frown creased her brow. Her weather-wise nostrils told her the darkening sky did not mean rain—and then she remembered hearing something about several strange dust-storms in the surrounding neighborhood territory....

" 'Twon't be rain—we're in for a pesky duster," she announced when she returned to the kitchen. And then, because dust-storms always bothered her severely, she closed the windows and doors and put on a sort of half-mask which Emmet, her husband, had made to help her breathe when the dust-laden wind was too strong for her delicate nose and throat. With this she was ready.

Even then, she could not keep away from the window; could not resist watching the approach of this unpleasant visitation. This storm was most unusual, she noticed at once. It had come up out of a clear sky and would very quickly blot out the noon-day sun—and yet it was not horizon-dimming, as dust-storms usually were. The distant horizon was clear on every side. It was just overhead that the oncoming darkness hovered—until suddenly a thick, smoke-like cloud swooped down and quickly blotted out everything outside. An inky-dark smokiness that came right into the house, through every little crevice.

That was plenty for Mary Reid; she took refuge in the cellar, amid the good-natured joshing of her friends. Only Luella followed her below and closed the door after them so that the all-invading dust would not find its way downstairs.

"You can't stay down here, mother," she protested. "This storm may take hours—days, for all we know. It *would* just have to come today!"

She stamped her foot in vexation—and the sound seemed to be echoed by a thump on the floor above them. Mother and daughter eyed each other questioningly—and the strange thump was repeated; three or four of them in a row. But this time Mary Reid knew what those sounds meant; they were the dull thuds of falling bodies!

Her legs were trembling oddly as she started toward the stairs, and then her feet seemed glued to the floor, her muscles turned to stone. That was the sound of footsteps upstairs—heavy footsteps coming in through the kitchen doorway. Footsteps—and no voices; which meant it was none of the men-folk come home....

Her legs might tremble and her knees might knock, but Mary Reid came from pioneer American stock. Masking her nose and mouth firmly, she crept noiselessly to the top of the steps and pressed one eye close to a crack in the door—to gaze at a sight that terrified her.

There, in her familiar kitchen, were half a dozen strangely uniformed, grotesquely gas-masked figures—and they were bending over the bodies of her friends who lay sprawled on the floor! They had what looked like hypodermic needles in their hands—needles that they drove deep into the women's necks! **BARELY IN** time she choked back the scream that welled up in her throat—and then she almost lost her balance on the steps. One after the other, the women were getting to their feet, were standing there meekly, dumbly, until one of the gas-masked figures opened the kitchen door and gestured toward it. Without a word, their faces expressionless masks, Hattie Sanderson and her seven neighbors filed out into the inky blackness!

Terrified and clutching each other for comfort, Mary Reid and her daughter cowered in the cellar for nearly fifteen minutes; until they could see through a low window that the darkness had thinned and then disappeared entirely. Not until then did they gather sufficient courage to creep upstairs and go to a window—to find the sun again shining brightly and every vestige of the smoke cloud gone.

Hesitantly Mary Reid opened the door and went outside, but nothing seemed to be changed. Everything seemed again normal, except that the darkness that had shrouded the sky had disappeared—and there was no trace of the eight women. They and the queer, gas-masked creatures with whom they had left had disappeared as if the earth had suddenly swallowed them up.

An oppressing sense of loneliness came over Mary Reid when she went back into the kitchen, a strange premonition that she would never see those friends again. Suddenly the world seemed to have become very empty, and she watched the road anxiously for sign of a human face. But there was not a soul; not a soul for more than two hours—and then a low dust cloud appeared on the northern horizon.

The men coming back from Tyndall! But that dust cloud came on slowly; far too slowly to have been raised by cars, or even horses....

Once more that curious sense of foreboding came over her, and she called Luella into the house. Together they watched the approaching dust cloud from behind the protection of the curtains at an upstairs window. And again they were in for a shocking surprise. Those were men, Mary Reid made out with field-glasses when they were still far in the distance. Marching men—with others who were on horseback riding beside them. A long column of men, marching four abreast; several hundred, at least.

At last they came sufficiently close so that she could begin to recognize some of their faces—and a gasp burst from her lips. Emmet was there among them, and so was Luella's young husband, Owen. One by one, she picked out her neighbors; but there were many others—the whole male population of Tyndall and the surrounding country!

Like automatons they marched along, unsmiling, saying not a word to one another—like slaves being herded and supervised by those mounted men. Those mounted men—they seemed to be Orientals of some sort; and they wore uniforms like the gas-masked men who had been there in her kitchen!

Now that strange column was just coming around the turn in the road, was passing the R-in-a-Box. Meekly, abjectly, they plodded listlessly—and neither Emmet nor Owen so much as turned their eyes toward their home as they passed it. Neither gave the faintest sign of recognition when Shep, the collie, ran out barking to meet them—and came slinking back to the house with head down and tail dragging.

That was too much for Luella.

"Mother!" her tense voice half-sobbed from between her ashen lips. "What has happened to them? Oh, my God! Ow—"

Just in time Mary Reid clapped her hand over her daughter's lips and smothered that tortured cry; held the struggling girl firmly, while she watched those mounted men in wide-eyed anxiety. But they had not heard Luella's half-voiced scream. Silently that weird column plodded past—and Mary Reid felt that she must be having a nightmare; felt that she must wake up and find that this whole weird day was nothing more than a bad dream.

Not until she had run into another room on the opposite side of the building and watched the dust cloud disappear down the road did she realize that they actually were gone. It was no dream; she *had* seen them. Emmet and young Owen—they were gone. They would never come back....

For long, endless hours the two women sat alone, left behind by a world that seemingly had passed them by. First their friends had been taken from them, then their husbands—and now they were alone, utterly alone.

Luella could not seem to comprehend it. At first she gave way to a wild paroxysm of grief. Then she sat like one stunned. But her mother rallied from the shock more quickly. The men-folks were gone, taken somewhere against their will—and Mary Reid was going out to find them!

To take her mind off the maddening thoughts that obsessed it, she made very thorough preparations. Men's clothing for both Luella and herself, revolvers for both of them, flashlights because she would not dare to travel until dusk, a pair of the best horses to be watered and fed and then saddled. At last she was ready, and by then Luella had gotten control of herself and promised to be as calm and dependable as her mother.

IN EARLY dusk they started cross-country, keeping to ground from which they could watch the road as they headed for the Circle S. Night had almost fallen when they rode up to the dark ranch-house, but even before they approached it they knew that the place was deserted. Hattie Sanderson had walked out of Mary's kitchen into the artificial night, and Lon had been one of that weirdly dead-alive column.

It was the same at three other places they tried. Empty, deserted homes everywhere. It seemed that all the world had been desolated; that only they two were left alive in it.

Mile after mile, with never the sign of another human being. Now it was thoroughly dark; a moonless night lit only faintly by the stars. Darkness on every side; so much of it that Mary began to feel that all light had gone out of the world—until, at last, she caught a twinkle and then a dull glow far ahead. That gave them fresh impetus, made them urge the horses on, until they could see that the light came from what appeared to be a huge encampment... light from lanterns and blazing fires.

Mary Reid rode as close as she dared. Then they dismounted

and ground-hobbled the horses, to go ahead stealthily on foot. Now she could see that the encampment was even larger than it had appeared; fully a quarter mile long, she judged. Most of the light was shielded from the outside by a sort of wall—a wall that was composed of hundreds of huge airships! Mighty, towering air-monsters that were many times larger than the greatest transport planes she had ever read about or seen illustrated. They were drawn around in a great circle, and in its center were hundreds of those Orientals; hundreds of the gas-mask men, with their masks hanging like extra heads over their shoulders.

"Japanese!" Luella whispered.

Hundreds—no, thousands—of Japanese there in the middle of a South Dakota prairie! Then America must be at war—and Emmet and Owen were prisoners somewhere in that huge camp. What other explanation could there be? Mary Reid asked herself.

Warily she led the way along the line of planes with the stealth of an Indian; two silently moving forms that were part of the blackness of the night. Keenly her eyes probed between the planes, and now she saw that there were women in that camp— and the hot blood rushed into her cheeks. American women, young and old, the playthings and the menial drudges for those yellow-skinned foreigners! So that was what had become of Hattie Sanderson and the others....

At the farthest end of the great encampment they found the section occupied by the white men. Rows and rows of them sat on the ground, regarding one another listlessly; as if they were no more than breathing corpses propped up there on the prairie floor. There were thousands of them, too; men of all ages and all professions—but Mary Reid's sharp eyes found her men-folk in all that silent assemblage.

The Tyndall men were all grouped more or less together, not far from the plane barrier. They could have gotten up and run and out in the darkness in a few moments… and the fact that they were allowed to sit there so close to freedom stabbed into Mary's heart the realization of their utter helplessness. They were chained there by something far stronger than physical bonds.

CAUTIOUSLY, FOOT by foot, the two women crept toward them. Between two of the great planes, and then forward into the enclosure, taking advantage of a patch of darkness that allowed them to get within twenty feet of their men. Mary dared go no closer.

"Emmet," she called. Softly at first, and then louder, more daring. "Emmet! Over this way. This is Mary, Emmet!"

But not a muscle of his face, lighted by a near-by campfire, moved. Straight ahead, he stared, unseeing, unhearing.

"Owen—Owen, darling!" Luella's agonized voice broke the terrible stillness that followed her mother's futile attempt. "I've come for you, Owen—over here in the shadow. You must hear me—you *must*, Owen!"

But, like his father-in-law, Owen Lockwood seemed utterly helpless, a man in a stupor or a trance. That was too much for his young wife. Mary Reid heard her daughter's heart-rending sob—and then the girl leaped to her feet and ran forward, to throw her arms frantically around her husband.

67

"Owen, darling!" she sobbed madly. "You *must* hear me! You *must* come with me! I'll make you!"

Her lips were against his face, showering him with kisses as her tears wet his cheeks; but Owen Lockwood might as well have been an inanimate doll in her arms. He did not seem to hear her, to be aware of her presence—but now the Japanese guards were. That end of the camp had seemed to be unpatroled, but suddenly half a dozen of the squatly built yellow men materialized from nowhere, and others came running from every direction.

They seized Luella and tore her away from her husband, but now she was a regular wildcat, clawing and tearing at them— until they mercilessly hammered her into submission.

Mary Reid's finger tightened on the trigger of her weapon as she watched their fists brutally pound the girl, drag her off by the yellow men in their own section of the camp. There were six bullets in that revolver—and Mary Reid was an expert markswoman. Six of those yellow devils she could have drilled through the head—but there might be six thousand of them in that camp.

Tears ran down her cheeks and her lips moved soundlessly as her trigger-finger relaxed and the revolver slipped back into its holster. She had no right to glut her vengeance, no right to throw away her own life by such an onslaught. Too much depended, now, on her getting away from that camp alive. Emmet, Owen, Luella, the Sandersons and all the other helpless friends in that huge camp—their fate depended upon her; yes, and perhaps the fate of all America....

Aghast with horror at what had befallen her loved ones, Mary Reid backed through the shadows cautiously, out between the two planes and into the night. Like a stunned creature she made her way across the fields until she reached the hobbled horses, mounted one of them, and picked a course that skirted wide around the invaders' camp.

One thing she must do, she kept telling herself over and over; she must bring help. Help? But where? Where in all South Dakota could she hope to raise a force that would be able to cope with that huge Japanese air armada? Where could she hope to find men who would not flee from the very mention of that powerfully armed force that was sweeping down on them?

The sheriff? The constables in Yankton? A derisive, half-hysterical chuckle escaped from her lips at that very thought! Even the governor; if he called out the state militia—what hope would those ground-tied boys have against those mighty aerial fortresses?

There was no hope in all South Dakota—but in that moment one name flashed into her mind. Operator 5! The man who had saved America when the odds seemed overwhelming and utter defeat seemed inevitable; the man who could perform miracles when other men were discouraged and defeated; the man who was ready at all times to defend America and American citizens no matter how powerful the threatening aggressor. Operator 5 would come to her rescue—if only she could reach him.

But she *must* reach him! She *must!* That thought pounded through her brain throughout the whole forty miles to Yankton; pounded and pounded and pounded, until it had become a chant, a monomania. Operator 5… she must reach Operator 5….

IT WAS long after midnight when she galloped her jaded horse into Yankton, but there were still lights in the courthouse. Two deputies were sitting and talking in the sheriff's office when she burst into it—a wild-eyed, haggard-faced woman, who was covered from head to foot with dust.

"Operator 5—I have to reach Operator 5!" the words parroted from her dry lips. "Operator 5, you understand—I have to talk to Operator 5."

"Sure, mother," one of the deputies soothed as he brought up a chair for her. "We'll get Operator 5 for you—but, you know, we'll have to give him sort of a little idea what it's about before he comes way out here. Maybe if we knew why you wanted him!"

"The Japanese—thousands of them—with hundreds of big airships! They have my man and my daughter." Mary Reid struggled desperately to be coherent. "They are out on the meadow twenty miles south of Tyndall, and they have everybody there— everybody is captured. The whole country back there is empty— all prisoners in the Japanese camp. I have to reach Operator 5, I tell you—he'll know what to do!"

Over her head the deputies exchanged winks.

"All right, mother," the spokesman nodded agreement. "We'll get him for you—but that'll take time, you know. Couple hours, probably. Why don't you try to sleep for a while; you look fagged. We'll call you as soon as we get him on the wire."

He sat down at the desk and started telephoning, and Mary Reid, hardly knowing what she was doing, allowed herself to be led off to a little room with a bed and a chair in it. Not until after the deputy was gone and the door had closed after him did her whirling brain begin to function with something like normalcy. And then she realized what had happened to her. They had not believed a word she told them—had put her in a detention room, a cell, after making that bluff at calling Operator 5!

At first she raved like a madwoman, pounding on the door and demanding to be released; and then her harried nerves gave way and she burst into hysterical tears....

But back in the sheriff's office, her fantastic story had planted a seed of doubt. Laughing at himself as he did so, one of the deputies tried to get Tyndall on the long distance telephone— and there was no answer. Puzzled, he tried several other towns in the vicinity—and the result was the same in every case.

"Probably a breakdown in the system," his partner suggested.

They clung to that possibility until morning, but then it was established that there was no line trouble. The Tyndall area and a large section of the state to the north of the town could not be reached by telephone or telegraph; did not even answer the calls of amateur radio operators. By that time Mary Reid was out of her cell and repeating every detail of her remarkable story over and over. Skeptical but impressed, the sheriff called on Roger Hawkins, a local airplane owner who occasionally assisted him in emergency scouting.

"Sounds like a crazy yarn, but maybe you'd better have a look at that section she talks about," he suggested doubtfully. "Fly over the place where she says she saw this camp—and then go on up to Tyndall and see why they don't answer their telephones." Roger Hawkins took off half an hour later—and that was the last Yankton ever saw of him. After he had been gone fifteen minutes his voice came back to their listening receivers through the ether.

"Approaching the site of that supposed encampment," he clipped. "The country around here seems deserted—no sign of life. There is some sort of camp there—a huge thing. Yes, there are planes. I see them taking to the air. They have spotted me—coming after me now! The sky is black with them! Over my head. I can't see! I—"

The last word was a scream—and after that there was silence.

Silence in the crowded sheriff's office, too—until someone ran out into the street and shouted the news. Hundreds of Japanese airplanes in the air, not forty miles away! Like wildfire panic swept the town, and half an hour later it was utterly deserted; every man, woman and child was fleeing frantically to the south.

But before she would leave in the sheriff's car, Mary Reid insisted on sitting down at his phone and putting through a call to Sioux City; from there to Washington. Not until she had been connected with Operator 5's office and had gasped out her amazing story was she willing to leave—and then she only went because the sheriff reminded her that her life was still of great value; that her work had only begun....

JOHN CHRISTOPHER was in charge in Operator 5's office when Mary Reid's telephone call was put through, and as he listened to her startling message his old eyes blazed and his pulses leaped with the call to action. The Japanese were in South Dakota! And Jimmy was desperately battling the plague they had let loose in California! Both attacks obviously were part of the same campaign, a concerted attack on America!

Or was this telephone call from South Dakota a fake? Or was the supposed invasion nothing but a decoy, intended to draw Operator 5 away from Los Angeles so that the way would be clear for the Japanese invaders?

John Christopher could only sit there and conjecture—and wish that he was twenty years younger. In the days when he was known as Q-6 on the roll of American Intelligence, he would have leaped into the fray with alacrity. That was before a bullet lodged in his body and stayed there, so close to his heart that any undue exertion might mean his sudden death. Since then, his had had to be the quiet role, the liaison man who could only act as contact—and send others to their deaths.

This telephone call from Mary Reid was right in line with other queer and disturbing rumors that had been coming in from the South Dakota area during the past few days. Rumors of strange midday darkness that had come and gone like a flash; jumbled tales from people who had seen the phenomenon from afar but could give little information about it. This was the first actual eye-witness account.

"But the whole thing may be nothing but a ruse," he shook his head worriedly. "I don't dare try to get in touch with Jimmy until we know conclusively just what there is to it."

"You will know that by tomorrow, Dad," his daughter Nan, who was a twin of Operator 5, said quietly. "I'll go up there with Danny Hickman. We'll see what's what and fly out over this supposedly invaded area if what we hear seems to warrant that. I'll call Danny now."

John Christopher's lips opened, half-parted to refuse to let her go; but they closed again and he nodded understanding. Well he knew how useless it was to try to curb either of these chips off the old block when their country needed them. The call of the service was in their blood—and, he admitted proudly, he would not have had it otherwise....

Nan Christopher and Dan Hickman made the trip from Washington in one of the speediest army scout planes, and they were in Sioux City by late afternoon. By then, the news of Yankton's frantic evacuation had spread throughout the surrounding territory, and village after village was being deserted. The roads to the south were swarming with cars of every sort, and Sioux City, itself, was on the verge of panic.

"We'll have a look at that area, Danny," Nan decided, after she had had a talk with Mary Reid and the sheriff from Yankton. "But we'll have to wait a bit. Night flying is the answer—or we'll meet the same fate as Roger Hawkins. Even so, I think we had better take out a bit of insurance against that."

The "insurance" took the form of a young Army Signal Corps lieutenant who was at Nan's side in the rear cockpit when the plane was ready to take off. At eleven o'clock Dan Hickman, at the controls, gave the engine the gun; and the dark ship sailed up into the black night. Toward the northwest they headed, and the last lights soon faded behind them as they passed over a country that was as abysmally dark as if no human being inhabited it for miles in every direction.

Peering down through their field-glasses, Nan and the lieu-tenant could not pick out the tiniest speck of light in all that territory—until they reached deserted Yankton. Then, a few miles behind the town, they caught the first gleam, which soon broke up into several spots of light.

"Here's where you get off, Lieutenant," Nan directed, as she gripped Hickman's shoulder to slow down until the officer could adjust his parachutes securely and bale out over the side.

Once more the plane resumed its course, straight for that clump of lights; mere dots which gradually began to take on the appearance of campfires, the heart of a great encampment. Slowing his motor so that it would be practically noiseless from below, Hickman cruised almost directly above the camp, while Nan stared through her glasses with incredulous eyes.

Everything Mary Reid had said was true; more than true. Every....

Suddenly her eyes jerked up from the glasses; her heart seemed to stop beating. The motor had gone dead! Dan Hick-man was working frantically at the controls. The plane was glid-ing, losing altitude—and then it was as if a magnet took hold of them and turned them around, changed their direction and headed them straight for that camp!

"I can't do a thing with it!" Hickman gasped. "The motor is stalling—some sort of ray from below, I'm afraid. The thing has hold of us. It's bringing us down. We're in for it, Nan—work fast!"

With all his skill he fought the ship—while Nan swiftly uncovered a magnesium beacon, worked on it for a moment and sent its bright red beam spearing high into the sky. Dot and dash, dot and dash, she broke that beam in the Morse code and flashed out a message that was only half-completed when Hickman managed to bring the ship down just outside the ring of air-monsters that towered over it.

Out from those ships scores of Japs came running, their flashlights playing on the helpless plane; but Danny Hickman was ready for them.

"Carry on, Nan!" was his good-by—and then he was over the side, charging straight at them, blazing away with two automatics, dodging and twisting, dropping to the ground and staggering back to his feet again.

The roar of shots dinned into her ears, but Nan was protected by the motor. None of them reached her, and she stayed at her task until the Japanese came swarming over the sides and knocked the beacon from her hands. The message was all but complete by then—and brave Danny Hickman was a bloody, bullet-sieved corpse on the ground.

"Nobly done, Danny!" she whispered his epitaph as her captors dragged her past his still body and across the camp into the presence of their commander, General Hachibu Aiko, of the Imperial Japanese Army.

CHAPTER 5
THE KNOW-NOTHING MEN

LOS ANGELES was a smouldering ruin, but it was worthless to the Japanese, who had paid with thousands of lives to take it. Due to the noble efforts of Mayor Hunter and his leper companions, the Japanese had been so crippled by that unexpected setback that they had been unable to press their attack any farther before the new American defense line was fully manned and ready for them.

Shells from the battleships occasionally landed in the long lines of entrenchments, but they did little damage and were far too costly a method of bombardment. The Japanese invasion was at a standstill, and the ring of fortifications that surrounded the devastated area was become more impregnable daily. Moto Taronago had failed miserably.

"We've licked them, Governor!" Operator 5 shook hands with Governor Knowlton in the foothills defense headquarters, as the chief executive of California came to attend a staff meeting. "We've checked their invasion and we've frustrated their diabolical attempt to spread a devastating plague throughout the nation. Taronago must be a decidedly discomfited individual at the present moment—but we must not let success go to our heads. That may be just what he is waiting for—what he is counting on.

"The moment after victory is always the most dangerous; that is when to look for the counter-attack—from an unexpected quarter," he again preached his doctrine of eternal vigilance. "We must be on the watch, night and day, ready at any moment to meet another emergency—"

Only Fate, the master stage director, could have timed so perfectly the telephone call that interrupted that little headquarters council.

"It is for you, Operator 5," one of the staff officers handed the instrument to Jimmy. "From Washington."

Even before he lifted the receiver to his ear, Jimmy Christopher felt a tingle of apprehension course through him. Perhaps it was the memory of the words that had just left his lips; perhaps a sudden realization that the Yellow Vulture, subtle conqueror of all Asia, was not a man to be beaten so easily. And the instant he caught the anxious ring in his father's voice he knew that his foreboding was all to well substantiated.

"Jimmy, I have bad news for you—the worst kind of news," John Christopher told him quickly. "The Japanese have landed in the Middle West with an air armada. They have conquered all of both the Dakotas and are moving forward to the south and east. The thing was accomplished so swiftly and so mysteriously that we heard nothing of it until the blighted area had reached almost to the southern border of South Dakota.

"And truly a blighted area it is! What sort of weapons they are using, we do not know, but they are stripping the territory of its population as they advance. Our people are being enslaved, men and women both; being turned into mindless creatures that seem to be like zombies, helpless to do anything but obey the orders they are given. Thousands of them are marching behind the huge war-planes that lead the way with some sort of blinding gas attack. We are rushing troops to try to stop them—but every man they capture is another they can use against us."

Another Japanese invasion that was sweeping down through the very center of America, just when it seemed that Moto Taronago's threat had been well disposed of! Another attack—

MOTO
TARONAGO

with weapons which the wily Japanese had not even used here in California!

Jimmy Christopher's face blanched as that stunning report came over the wire, and as he realized its significance. This

California attack, this threat of a plague that would sweep the nation—they had been nothing more than feints; nothing more than attempts to hold the nation's attention and sap its strength—while the real onslaught got under way in the Middle West. Instead of winning this Japanese war almost before it started, they had won nothing more than a preliminary skirmish—and had lost invaluable time in doing so!

"Nan flew over their camp and was brought down," John Christopher was saying. "She got a message off to a Signal Corps man before they silenced her, but he had great difficulty getting back with it. He lost twenty-four hours, and during that time the Japanese came out into the open and are sweeping everything before them."

"Nan—is she all right?" Jimmy inquired anxiously for the twin with whom he had shared so much in common ever since their birth.

"God knows, Jimmy," his father's voice was low, husky. "She had almost finished her beacon message when it was cut short. The Japs were closing in on her—and after that we heard nothing."

NAN IN the hands of those Japanese invaders.... In the hands of unscrupulous fiends like the Yellow Vulture.... As Operator 5 dropped the receiver back onto its hook her face, so like his own, seemed to be looking at him expectantly from the hazy distance. Into his mind crowded memories of the times without number when they had stood together, the times when she had gladly risked her life for him, when she had rushed into deadly peril in order to save him from danger.... And now she needed him—perhaps more than ever before in her adventurous life....

Rapidly he broke the news to the others and outlined the plans that were formulating in his racing brain.

"I doubt that you will have much more trouble here," he finished, "but you will have to be prepared every moment. As long as that fleet remains on this side of the Pacific there is danger. But General Butler—" he nodded to the grizzled army commander of the Pacific Coast Division—"will know how to handle that. I am flying to Nebraska immediately—with my personal staff," he half-smiled as he turned to where Diane and Tim Donovan were eyeing him anxiously. "We will take off as soon as a plane is ready."

The governor and most of the staff officers followed him out to the improvised flying field with their good wishes and farewells, and when they arrived at the big bombing plane that was already being warmed up he noticed that Diane and Tim Donovan had an escort of their own—one who made them look like children beside him.

"Seven feet of man—I guess that wouldn't be much of a help in a flying trip, would it, Operator 5?" Gorilla Cagle grinned when he caught Jimmy's eyes upon him. "I sure would like to go with you, though. Since the little lady, there, saved me from what happened to all those others in the studio I sorta felt that she has a little coming to her that'll take me a long time to pay back. Sometimes seven feet of man isn't a bad thing to have around—with the sort of ruckuses she gets into."

Jimmy had noticed the dog-like devotion with which the

giant kept his eyes on Diane; and suddenly it occurred to him that a bodyguard such as this might be just what she needed to keep her safe.

"Okay, Seven Feet," he laughed, "hop in. You're going along."

THE WAVE of American refugees had reached a point about fifty miles north of Omaha when Operator 5's plane arrived on the scene. Prepared as he was for disaster, he was appalled at the debacle that confronted him. Thousands of families, carrying what they could of their household possessions, were pouring in frantic streams to the south, east and west, the specter of awful fear stark in their wide-staring eyes. At their rear, a makeshift army was frenziedly digging in; throwing up trenches that the diggers knew would be next to useless when the Japanese armada swept down upon them. The hopelessness of resistance, the foreknowledge of certain defeat—that was what was taking the will to fight from these men. They were beaten before the enemy approached, and they knew it.

"It is this infernal gas they use," General Sidney Morrell, who was commanding the defense, complained bitterly as he watched his laboring men. "It gets in everywhere—even through many of our gas-masks, and it knocks the men out immediately. But even when we are able to withstand the gas, we face the necessity of shooting down our own people—thousands of helpless Americans, men and women, who come on like automatons. It's like slaughtering children to kill them—and yet our men know that the same fate awaits them if they are captured."

"This automaton set-up—have you any idea how it is effected, General?" Jimmy asked.

"I wish to God I knew that, Operator 5," Morrell sighed. "Some sort of hellish injection they shoot into captives which deprives them of all will-power, all initiative—apparently."

"That's a job for Doc King," Jimmy said promptly. "Get a wire off to him, Tim. Tell him we need him here immediately."

But there was not time for him to wait for Norman King, the head of his scientific research laboratories, to arrive. Every hour was important in checking the spreading invasion—and every minute might decide Nan Christopher's fate, if it had not already been decided. Jimmy interviewed first Mary Reid and then Wharton, the Signal Corps man, and learned from them what he could of the topography of the country to the north. Not a word had been heard from Nan since her magnesium flare blinked out on the edge of the enemy's camp. Either she was a prisoner in that camp—perhaps a helpless automaton like the others—or she was dead.

"I am going to find out which," Jimmy decreed—and firmly vetoed Tim Donovan's demand to go along. "I want you to stay here and work with King, when he arrives," he directed. "Gene Nesbitt and Tom Cahill will go in with me."

Nesbitt and Cahill were two of Operator 5's most dependable agents. Veterans of many a desperate campaign, they had proved their courage and resourcefulness when the failing of either would have meant sure death.

"I am going out there into the invaded territory just as I am— as Operator 5," Jimmy outlined his quickly formed plan, and nodded his head when he saw their unconcealed surprise. "That's a gamble, I know, but I think it ought to work. Undoubtedly this Japanese commander has been in constant touch with Moto Taronago and knows of the impersonation of me Taronago engineered in Los Angeles. That masquerade was so excellent that it almost fooled my closest friends—so I am going to spring it on the Japs. I am going in there as their confederate, the fake Operator 5 who has been working with them!

"I want half an hour's start. Then you fellows come in after me and keep in my rear, ready in case I need your help in getting out—or in getting Nan out, should I not be able to come back with her."

Nesbitt and Cahill nodded grim understanding....

IT WAS morning when Operator 5 started out into the occupied territory, early morning when the dawn was just lifting. By the time the sun was fully risen he was miles into the deserted area that, only a few days before, had been a thriving countryside. Even now, the isolated homes and the little villages he passed looked as if their inhabitants were still asleep—except that there was already about them that indefinable air of desolation that attaches immediately to a place that has been abandoned.

Houses with the doors and windows all closed—and no plume of smoke going up from the chimneys; stores with the doors locked. Show-windows in wild disorder as the proprietors had hurriedly stripped them of the most valuable and easily transportable merchandise; barns with closed doors, and no horses or cattle in the fields. All were the unmistakable signs of a countryside that had been yielded to the invader. And every so often there was a place with the doors still ajar, with odds and ends of furniture on the porch or strewn on the ground—abandoned when the frantically fleeing owners had found that they could not manage to take everything with them.

Those mute evidences of pathetic tragedy stabbed at Jimmy's heart and forged anew his bitter hatred for the avaricious coveters of world power who deliberately inflicted such misery on an unoffending people!

Prepared with a carefully tested gas mask for the coming of the enemy planes, he kept scanning the sky to the north, watching for their advent—but it was not until after ten o'clock that he spied the telltale smudge in the sky that was the forewarning of their arrival. Rapidly it drew nearer, became a dense cloud of smoke that concealed the ships completely. But he was ready for it when it passed over him.

Crouching in the protection of a small thicket close to an abandoned farmhouse, he lay still while the darkness closed above him; waited until the enveloping blanket had lifted and he could see the oncoming lines of American captives less than a quarter mile away. Closely he studied them through his glasses—and was shocked at their blank, expressionless faces, at the mechanical precision with which they plodded along.

These men and women were like robots! They seemed to be able to do nothing but trudge forward blindly—until they approached the nearby farmhouse and tragedy erupted right in their path.

At that unfortunate moment a door in the ground opened up—and out staggered a half-stupefied family. A root cellar, Jimmy identified their refuge; this family must have been delayed in getting away from their home. They had waited too long and had fled to the underground vegetable store-house when the threatening cloud appeared in the sky—but they had come out at the very worst moment!

An old man and his wife, two young women and a man who seemed to be the husband of one of them…. Jimmy saw them stagger out and weave groggily toward the building. The younger man's wife clutched a baby to her breast, and a child of about three clung to her skirt. That much he saw—and then the advancing line was upon them!

With mechanical, unhurried movements the automatons went into action. They seized the old couple and one of the younger women, but the young mother screamed and took to her heels. Half a dozen of those silent, expressionless robots went after her. There was something weirdly terrifying about the irresistibility of their movements, but the young husband flung himself in their path, strove desperately to fight them off.

That valiant stand lasted but a moment; then he was seized and was overwhelmed, tied up and dropped to the ground while another half dozen took after his wife and overhauled her before she could reach the building. She screamed shrilly and fought like a madwoman—but they ripped the child from her arms and tossed it on the ground as if it were a bundle of rags!

Their orders were to discard or do away with the children, Jimmy realized with a surge of horror. The Japanese wanted only the men and women, only more recruits for this eerie army of automatons! Helpless in their hands, the young mother was just about to be tied up—when one of them struck out brutally at the three-year-old who still clung to her skirts. The blow just missed, but the child flew in terror, her pursuer after her—and in her frenzied anxiety the mother tore herself free and joined the chase.

Straight toward Jimmy Christopher's hiding place they came—and in that moment he fought a furious battle with himself. He had no right to interfere, he told himself doggedly. He had no right to jeopardize his mission, no right to endanger what he might be able to accomplish for the whole nation. But he could not see that child mercilessly cut down; could not stand by and see that young mother killed in her effort to protect the babe!

Just as one of the blank-faced robots was about to seize the girl, Jimmy sprang out and thrust him aside; lashed out with his automatic and knocked down two others who had grabbed the mother.

"Stop it!" he roared at them. "She is a woman—and you are men! She is an American, like yourselves!"

But they paid no attention. They closed in on him, lackluster eyes turned to him from blank, emotionless faces. Somehow he *must* make them understand! Desperately he dived at one who seemed to have been a man of intelligence, grabbed him and shook him, slapped his face smartly and peered into his eyes.

"Listen, man!" Jimmy barked at him. "This is Operator 5—understand that? Operator 5! No matter what you have been told to do, I am changing those orders. You are an American—not a slave of the Japanese! An American, understand? An *American!*"

But the word seemed to have no significance whatever for the

87

man. As Jimmy stared into those expressionless eyes he doubted that he was even heard, and if he was it was certain that his words reached an altogether dormant brain. The man struggled mechanically but irresistibly.

NOW THEY were all around Jimmy. He knew that it was useless to struggle; they were far too many for him. Quietly he let them tie him up and stretch him on the ground with the others—and tried to steel his ears to the pitiful screams of the young mother; tried not to think of what must have happened to that innocent child.

Helplessly he lay there for perhaps twenty minutes, and then a party of Japanese came along. One after the other, they bent over the tied-up captives and pressed a hypodermic needle into their necks; inoculated them with something that put an end to their struggles—that silenced the young mother's screams, and reduced her to stolidity. Meekly the captives rose and stood waiting, when their bonds had been cut.

Then it was Jimmy's turn, but before they could jab the needle into his neck he spoke to them quickly—in Japanese. "Careful—I am not one of these!" he warned the fellow who hovered over him. "I have just come from the American lines, an emissary from the Honorable Moto Taronago. I am on my way to your commander."

The magic name of the Yellow Vulture produced an immediate impression. The soldier drew back with his needle and called to another, a sergeant, who seemed to be in charge of the squad. This was a man of more intelligence, but the name of Taronago was equally potent with him. He ordered that Jimmy be released and detailed two of his men to take him to the rear, to the head-quarters of Hachibu Aiko.

Hachibu Aiko—that would be the test! On the way back to headquarters Jimmy used all his tact in drawing out his guards. At first they were reticent and suspicious, but gradually the sound of their own language and bits of information about the capture of Los Angeles began to have their effect. Gradually their tongues loosened, and by the time he reached headquarters Jimmy had a fair idea of Hachibu Aiko's background—and an all too vivid idea of the man's objective....

The general had established his headquarters in a large farmhouse that stood in the center of his camp. Hundreds of the Japanese planes must have gone forward in that great, sun-blackening wave that had passed over him, but Jimmy saw that there were still scores of them here in a skeleton formation of the last night's encampment—and the strength of this huge invading host appalled him.

Every available plane in America must be mustered to meet them. Every factory must be set to work at top speed produc-ing more and supplying them with the defensive and offensive weapons they would need. Already Operator 5 was planning the campaign he would launch the moment he got back to his own lines—and then he was ushered into Hachibu Aiko's presence.

The general, a round-faced, bullet-headed man of about fifty, sat at a large dining-room table, surrounded by his officers. His sharp, almond-shaped eyes looked up half-wonderingly, half-suspiciously at this newcomer who was of the race against which he was warring.

"Greetings, Honorable Hachibu Aiko," Jimmy Christopher bowed. "I believe perhaps you have had some news of my unworthy self—Operator 5?" He smiled broadly. "I have just come from the American lines above Omaha, after my work with the Honorable Moto Taronago in California was finished. The Americans have not the slightest suspicion that I am not the man I pretend to be. They ask my advice on everything—and will follow it profoundly. That may be quite advantageous to us, do you not agree?"

Hachibu Aiko did agree, that was quite apparent. The possibility of having the Americans blindly following orders which he would give appealed to him immensely. His questions were almost perfunctory; questions about the situation in California, which Jimmy could answer truthfully and accurately.

"That does not matter," the commander shrugged. "It was of no importance; and I did not approve of the plague myself. It is as well that it did not spread; the danger to our own men, when we subjugate the entire country, would have been too great. It is our offensive here that will bring this stubborn-necked country to its knees!"

On the table before him was spread a large map of the United States, with a great brown blot staining the upper part of the Middle West. Like water leaking through a ceiling and coming down on a wall, that blot just below the Canadian border was spreading in all directions. Jimmy was shocked at the extent of it—and appalled at the methodical precision with which these Orientals had mapped it for days to come. Like ripples caused by a stone that is tossed into a pool, each day's progress was laid out on that map—widening ripples that, at the end of a month, lapped over the Atlantic and the Pacific coasts and reached beyond the farthest tip of Texas!

One month—and Hachibu Aiko was expected to conquer America from coast to coast, from border to border!

"Excellent—excellent!" Jimmy pretended enthusiasm and admiration as he bent over that dismaying map. "There has been no trouble making the scheduled progress each day, I see." He shook his head in approval. "But we have had no real test yet—nothing like Los Angeles. Do you think, sir, that when we approach, say here—" his finger came down on Chicago—"it will be as easy as it has been so far? Is it not possible that there will be a more stubborn defense?"

"Let them defend stubbornly!" Hachibu Aiko laughed. "The more stubbornly the better. That will give us so many more men for our captive levies. But we are well prepared for Chicago—and for any other large city that may attempt to prove troublesome. Let them resist—and we will show them weapons such as they have never seen. Weapons which—"

It was at that point that an orderly appeared at the doorway and made an announcement that sent Jimmy Christopher's heart plummeting down into his shoes, that set his every nerve atingle.

"His Excellency, the Honorable Moto Taronago!" came sonorously in singsong syllables that seemed to be mockingly pronouncing his doom….

The Yellow Vulture—there at Hachibu Aiko's headquarters! Jimmy knew that his masquerade could not hope to stand that acid test. He set himself for the recognition that was inevitable; set himself to make a desperate break for freedom—or to take that vulturine-beaked fiend into death with him, if death it was to be....

Then Taronago was standing in the doorway, was bowing an acknowledgment of their salaams. His close-set eyes ran over the room's occupants swiftly—and passed over Jimmy as if his presence there was entirely natural and to be expected. Stepping forward, he shook hands with them, one after the other.

"And you, too, Operator 5," he smiled knowingly as his hands clasped Jimmy's—and so bafflingly was the man's enigmatical face that Jimmy could not tell whether he had been taken for *himself* or for the masquerader he was pretending to be!

Apparently Taronago had accepted him as the masquerader. That seemed incredible, and yet the Yellow Vulture seemed entirely unsuspicious. He chatted with Hachibu Aiko and his officers, told them of the events in California and made queries about the progress of the invasion.

It was not until the conversation turned to spies and the commander mentioned having captured the sister of the real Operator 5 that Taronago's beady eyes gleamed with an unholy light. Leaning close to Hachibu Aiko, he whispered softly—and when his eyes turned back to Jimmy, they were filled with gloating mockery....

CHAPTER 6
A NATION AT BAY

HER ALL-IMPORTANT message had gotten through to young Lieutenant Wharton and nothing else mattered, Nan Christopher had told herself as the Japanese overwhelmed her and dragged her into their camp. Wharton would have picked up her beacon flashes by now and would also get the message back to the American lines, to be relayed to Jimmy. America at least would realize the peril it faced. Beyond that, she had no hope.

Silently she stood before Hachibu Aiko when they brought her into his headquarters. Steadily she refused to answer his questions, until at last he shrugged in annoyance.

"Give her an injection and put her with the others," he ordered, as he turned back to his papers.

His interest in her was finished. He did not even watch as the hypodermic needle she dreaded was loaded and lifted to her throat—but just before the point pierced her skin one of his staff stepped up to the commander's desk.

"Your pardon, sir," he interrupted, "but I have just placed this woman. Her face was familiar to me, and now I know why. It is the face of Operator 5—and I recall also that this Operator 5 is said to have a twin sister. Undoubtedly this is she who has fallen into our hands."

"The sister of Operator 5?" Hachibu Aiko and the rest of his staff were interested immediately.

With the knowledge of her identity, it was to their advantage to keep her in full control of her senses. The hypodermic needle was waved away, and she was placed in a chair that they surrounded. For half an hour they kept her there, plying her with questions which she refused to answer, making her promises which she knew they would not keep, threats which she did not fear. No matter how they tried to make her divulge vital information and send back false messages to the American lines, she steadfastly refused.

"Perhaps you will change your mind if we give you a chance to think this over—with the proper companionship," Hachibu Aiko finally suggested, and then he turned to one of his officers. "Get me two of the men," he ordered. "Two who have no woman. They shall have *this* one."

Nan's cheeks flushed, and her hands became as cold as ice when two round-faced, grinning privates were brought into the room. Eagerly they accepted the prize and dragged her off to the small tent they shared. Two young Japanese who, Nan could see at once, were rather awe-stricken by this strange American woman they had surprisingly drawn.

They closed their tent flap and turned to her uncertainly, evidently ready for a furious battle. But when she smiled at one of them and went readily into his arms he seemed too astonished to know what to do. His partner, likewise, was nonplussed; could only stand there and grin foolishly as Nan submitted to the yellow man's clumsy embrace—until her fingers reached the knife she had spied at his belt.

In a moment her hand closed around it, and then it was out of its sheath, was pressed against his throat as her left hand searched beneath his jacket and came away clutching his Luger pistol. They could not understand her language, but they could understand the muzzle of that weapon.

"Back!" she spat at them. "Back!" And they retreated—promptly.

There was no chance to tie them up. All she could hope to do was open the flap of that tent and get outside, then to make a desperate break for freedom. Behind her back one hand fumbled with the tent fastening, got it open, and then she stepped out quickly into the darkness—and into the hands of four staff officers who seized and disarmed her!

Nan's hopes sank dismally as she realized that she had never had a chance; that wily Hachibu Aiko had only pretended to give her to those unsuspecting privates, hoping that she would break down and do as he wished.

"Your life could be made very much more pleasant if you were more sensible, young lady," he told her when she was brought back into his presence. "For the time being, you will be kept confined—until I decide on what will be the most effective way of changing your mind. When next I send for you—I do not believe that you will enjoy what follows." After that she was chained up securely in a room in one of the planes that was as strong as any prison cell. For three days she stayed there, seeing nobody but her jailer, who stayed well out of her reach. She felt the plane move from place to place, realizing that the invasion was going on unchecked despite her message. Knowing that she had failed....

IT WAS nearly noon on the fourth day when she was liber-

The next instant the firing-squad
was being bowled over!

ated. A squad of soldiers took her in charge and marched her out—and into her mind flashed Hachibu Aiko's warning that what was to follow would not be pleasant! Tensely she walked between them.

Headquarters was in a farmhouse this time. Up to the front door they marched her, and then two guards took her inside. When they led her into the commander's room she saw that his staff was gathered around him as before, but now there was another Oriental present—and from his vulturine profile she identified him at once. This must be Moto Taronago, the dreaded Yellow Vulture!

Fascinated, she stared at that predatory countenance—and was fully into the room before she saw that it had another occupant. Jimmy! Jimmy, sitting there with the others, as if he was one of them!

But almost instantly she sensed the tension of that strange gathering; almost instantly she saw that Taronago was watching Jimmy, also—was watching him wolfishly. Jimmy was equally aware of that keen-eyed scrutiny. He was doing his best to appear unconcerned; to look at her without betraying the slightest sign of recognition. And just as quickly she took her cue from him.

"So this is the young lady who will not talk," Taronago's voice was a silky purr. "Perhaps we can remedy that, General Aiko. I think that her own brother will be more than willing to convince her that her silence is very foolish. Operator 5," he turned to Jimmy, "I have a sister of my own; I know how stubborn they can be. Perhaps you can argue with her most convincingly with this—"

Broadly he winked at Jimmy, as if they shared the secret of Jimmy's masquerade and were fooling the girl with it. But in that moment Jimmy knew that the Yellow Vulture was well aware of his identity and intended to make him betray himself.

Out on the table Taronago placed a little leather case that contained a dozen bamboo wedges, each an inch and a half long, half an inch wide at one end and coming to a needle-sharp point at the other. With them was a small metal hammer and a sheaf of long-burning matches. A devilish torture outfit!

Her guards led Nan up to the table and pressed her right hand out flat on it, then turned it up at the knuckles so that her fingers were spread wide. Expectantly they turned to Jimmy.

"All right, Operator 5!" Taronago beamed.

Desperately Jimmy Christopher sought a way out of that hellish trap—but there was none. Nan, he could see, realized by now something of what was afoot; realized, at least, that this was an attempt to make him play into Taronago's hands—and she did not intend to let him do it.

"Please, Jimmy," she spoke to him soundlessly, barely moving her lips. "I can stand it. Please!"

Now every eye in that room was fixed on him. There was no more time for delay. He had to act—and he did. Picking up the little hammer, he took one of the bamboo slivers and stepped close to Nan, as if he intended to force the wedge beneath one of her fingernails and light it—but instead of that he suddenly whirled and hurled the hammer straight at Taronago's head and then leaped for the fellow.

That was hopeless, as Jimmy had known it would be. The

Yellow Vulture had been waiting for just such a break. Instantly Jimmy was seized from every side and was overpowered before he had covered half the distance that separated him from his grinning tormenter.

"This is the real Operator 5 you have been entertaining, General Aiko," Taronago exulted. "I have met the gentleman before, and on that occasion I promised myself that the next time we met would be the last. May I suggest that he be given to a firing-squad immediately? A firing-squad of his own people— he will appreciate that!" he added, as Hachibu Aiko nodded and gave the order.

A firing-squad of the know-nothing men!

Into the headquarters they marched, eight Americans with lackluster eyes and expressionless faces, under the command of a Japanese officer. Hard-eyed and tight-lipped, grimly averting his face from where Nan sobbed hysterically and fought desperately to break away from her guards, Jimmy took his place between their ranks and marched out of the house.

THE OFFICER led the way to a wall at one side of the building, escorted Jimmy to it, and lined up the firing-squad about twenty-five feet in front of him. Not until then had Jimmy had a chance to study the faces of all his executioners—and what he saw now almost jolted him out of his composure. Dull-eyed and expressionless like the rest, two of those men were Gene Nesbitt and Tom Cahill, the agents who were to have followed him into the invaded area!

For just an instant hope had leaped in his breast, but a second glance at those immobile faces dashed it to destruction. They, too, had fallen victim to this mind-deadening drug.

Now the Japanese raised his sword.

"Ready!" he barked. "Aim!"

But instead of a volley of shots, that fatal command brought swift action. A split-second before it left the officer's lips, Nesbitt and Cahill suddenly swung on their companions and charged them headlong, bowled them over before the know-nothing men could step out of the way. At the same instant a shot rang out from Cahill's gun, and the Japanese officer pitched forward.

"Okay, Operator 5!" Gene Nesbitt yelled—but his invitation was not needed; Jimmy had already gone into action....

Springing to the side of the dead officer, he grabbed the man's sword and pulled an automatic from its holster at his belt. With Nesbitt and Cahill at his side, he charged forward in a headlong dive for the door of the farmhouse, where Nan had been dragged to force her to watch her brother's execution.

One of the guards who held her died with two of Tom Cahill's bullets in his heart. Jimmy's sword clove through the skull of the other. Then Nan was free, was racing with the men in a mad rush for a motor truck that stood unguarded near the front of the building.

Nesbitt reached it first and sprang behind the wheel.

"In beside him, Nan!" Jimmy ordered, then he and Cahill flung themselves flat on the floor in back and poured a deadly fire into the ranks of the Japanese who came running to stop them.

Lead hailed against the truck's metal sides, but before the

bullets were able to do any harm Nesbitt got the machine under way—and they sped out onto the road that led toward the American lines. They were clear—but before they had gone more than three or four miles Jimmy saw that an armored car was pursuing them, a car that was faster than the truck. Nesbitt saw that, too, and crouched over the wheel, coaxing every possible bit of speed from the machine.

It was useless. The pursuing car was catching up steadily. It would be no more than a matter of four or five minutes now before it was abreast—and a volley of shots from behind those impregnable steel plates would end the chase. Jimmy eyed the pursuer bitterly. They were so close to freedom, it made losing out now all the more galling....

"Might as well turn off the road and make a stand," he shouted a few minutes later, when the oncoming car was within bullet range.

"There's a village just ahead here." Cahill cuddled his rifle and wasted a shot on the pursuers. "Ought to be there any minute now."

And then Jimmy saw it—a tiny village of no more than a dozen houses. Nesbitt must have been making for it as a last desperate resort, hoping to take refuge in one of the buildings, but now that was too late. The armored car was right on top of them; bullets were already spattering all around them—when suddenly the truck veered sharply to the left just as Nesbitt yelled, *"Jump!"* and pushed Nan off the seat.

Jimmy sprang clear as the truck swerved into the car's path, and Tom Cahill landed in the ditch beside him when the vehicles crashed. Head-on the armored car hit that truck and plowed half-way through it before the dead weight stopped it—half-way through what had been the truck's cab!

And Gene Nesbitt was still penned behind that wheel....

Operator 5 felt a lump rise in his throat as he realized what he had just witnessed. Gene Nesbitt had died gloriously in that collision; had deliberately yielded his life so that his chief might be spared to America.

But in the next few moments it seemed that his sacrifice would be in vain. The Japanese were pouring out of the stalled car—half a dozen of them were coming on with blazing guns.

Swiftly Jimmy lifted Nan to her feet and helped her out of the ditch. With the girl between them, he and Cahill headed for the nearest building—but they would never make it! The Japanese were kneeling, were taking deliberate aim that would not miss. Suddenly a blasting fire poured from one of those buildings. Roaring guns in front of them and more behind—they were caught between two fires! One minute more....

Grabbing Nan in his arms, Jimmy flung her to the ground beside him and whirled to confront this new menace; but that blistering hail of lead was passing far over their heads—and when he turned back to the Japanese four of them lay dead. The other two were staggering back to the protection of their car—only to be cut down and pitched to the ground before they had gone half a dozen steps!

CHAPTER 7
TEST OF COURAGE

T HE DISHEARTENED troops were in full retreat with the terrified populace, as Dr. Norman King arrived at the American lines in Nebraska. They had made a valiant stand in the entrenchments they had been constructing when Operator 5 went out into the deserted area, but once more the all-blinding darkness had come down to envelop and overcome them. And after that came the flesh-chilling lines of near-specters; walking corpses that a few days before had been stalwart American men and women, many of them soldiers with these same regiments.

The retreat had become a panic-stricken rout when King arrived on the scene; so bad that he and the army chauffeur who drove him had all they could do to defend the car which brought him from the nearby airport. Disdainfully the doctor glowered at what he considered the rankest sort of cowards, but when he reached headquarters and expressed his opinion General Morrell shook his head patiently.

"It isn't as simple as that, Doctor," he defended his men. "I know my troops. They will follow me into hell and stand against the devil himself if they think they have even half a chance. But here they know they have no chance. The threat of the Japanese, with their huge planes and their superior weapons, is bad enough—but what demoralizes the men is the prospect of being gassed and turned into one of those mindless creatures, to be shot down by their own people. When those waves of automatons come charging at them, our men see themselves in the places of the mindless victims they have to kill—for tomorrow they may be there, helpless puppets in the hands of the Japanese! That's enough to shatter any man's morale."

"And has nothing been done to combat this use of our own men against us?" Norman King asked. "Is there no way to appeal to them—to bring them back to normal?"

"That's why Operator 5 sent for you, Doctor King," the General told him earnestly. "We have had physicians trying to solve the problem, but they have gotten nowhere. The army of what we call the 'know-nothing men' is growing steadily, alarmingly. It is spreading out wider and wider as the Japanese cover more territory. In any other invasion the invading force has always been expected to lose a certain percentage of its enrollment with every advance—but in this case the ranks of the aggressors are constantly swelling, continually being augmented by the prisoners they take. I am no calamity-howler, Doctor—but unless this thing can be stopped, unless something can be done for these thousands of helpless prisoners in the Japanese ranks, there will be no stopping the invasion. It will spread over America from coast to coast!"

"Then we will stop it." From the lips of some men those words would have had the sound of braggadocio, but for Norman King they were simply the statement of a purpose, something which he would have to do. "First of all, General Morrell, I'll have to have some of these prisoners for study and experimentation—"

King's words stopped and his eyes lifted inquiringly as he noticed how the general's face had clouded.

"I feared you were going to ask that," Morrell admitted glumly. "We haven't any to give you, Doctor—and to get any for you is practically impossible. The lines of these brain-robbed captives always follow well in the rear of the Japanese planes and the sun-blotting darkness that comes with them—and by that time our men are just about finished. They are glad to escape with their lives—much less thinking about taking prisoners. To get a prisoner back through that barrage would take a regiment—and then I doubt that they would succeed."

"But I *must* have them or I can do nothing," Norman King expostulated. "Research depends upon experimentation. It is hopeless to even attempt that unless we have something on which to work. I *must* have some of those captives, General— at least one!"

"You will have him, Doctor," a voice from his side assured confidently. Tim Donovan had taken no part in this conversation, but now he stepped forward. "Operator 5 told me to see that you are supplied with anything you need—and if you need one of these captives, I'll get one for you. I won't need a regiment, General—" he turned to Morrell. "All I want is a squad of volunteers—"

"But you won't have a chance when the Japanese planes come over and lay down their barrage!" Morrell protested.

"Admitted," Tim nodded, "but I am not going to wait for them to come over. I am going in there now, prepared for their coming. I am going out to meet them and will take the know-nothing men by surprise—that is our only chance. Give me eight volunteers who are willing to go out with me, and I'll bring you your man."

"Getting you the volunteers will be the easiest part of it," the General assured; and it was.

Within ten minutes there were fifty men lined up at the headquarters' door; fifty men who were willing and anxious to walk into the jaws of death if by so doing there was a hope of putting an end to this terror that had robbed them of friends and relatives—and now threatened to steal away their very brains.

Tim Donovan interviewed them carefully, and the eight he chose were men in whose heart hatred for these yellow invaders blazed like a searing flame. Gilman and Mitchell, whose wives were somewhere in that Japanese camp; Sharp and Johnson, who were the only survivors of families the invaders had wiped out ruthlessly; the Shepard brothers, who had lost their homes and a profitable business, all that they had in the world, when the invaders swept through their town; Garland, who had served with Operator 5 many times before; and Dawson, an old-timer to whom the country into which they were going was as familiar as the palm of his hand.

WITH GAS-MASKS hanging ready on their chests, they started out—nine men who were going north when all the rest of the world seemed to be stampeding wildly to the south. Carefully Tim Donovan scanned the sky ahead of them, while Dawson led the way by a back-road shortcut that would strike the main road some miles south of where the enemy advance had last been known to halt. For more than an hour they pressed forward through the deserted countryside before that telltale

cloud again suddenly filled the sky far to the north and came on with incredible speed. They halted.

"Off the road—*quick!*" Dawson called to them. "There's a cut-bank creek over there less'n a quarter mile, and I know washed-out caves where they'll never think to look for us."

Before the planes droned overhead and the impenetrable darkness came down, they were gas-masked and ready, crouching in the shelter of the caves—and then the night closed in on them. To Tim, it seemed to last for hours; gloom so thick that he could not see his hand six inches in front of his face, gloom in which anything might be creeping up on him. Chills ran down his spine as he tensed and set himself for instant action should their hiding place be invaded—but gradually the gloom began to lift, to fade to a smoky gray, then to the hazy mist of early dawn.

"Now," he passed the word along to his men. "They ought to be here at any moment."

Cautiously they crawled from their covert and lay in a fringe of low brush that skirted the creek. The dark smudge that was the planes had disappeared to the south and the gray mist had almost lifted. Like dawn fog dissipated by the rays of the rising sun, it melted away—and there, no more than an eighth of a mile away, came the know-nothing men. Line after line of them, men and women together—thousands of poor, dazed creatures who marched like automatons.

Tim gasped as he saw their number—and realized that his plan would not work. To attempt to snatch a captive from those close-packed ranks was bound to mean failure and could result in nothing but the death of scores of these unthinking victims of Japanese fiendishness—as well as the annihilation or capture of his own little force.

Those eight volunteers must have realized that, too, but not one of them flinched. Crouched low in the bushes, they tensed as the steadily advancing lines came nearer, ready to leap forward in a desperate charge if he said the word—but Tim couldn't. He groaned inwardly as he recalled his confident promise to Norman King and realized how much depended upon its fulfill-ment. This was failure—but it was better than useless slaughter.

"It won't work, men," he called softly through the bushes. "It would be only murder to shoot them down, and we'd never get through. Fall back into the caves—and we'll see if any of them follow us in there."

That would be the solution. But the know-nothing men were not very thorough searchers; they overwhelmed anyone in their path, but they did not have the initiative to hunt out possible fugitives who might be in hiding. From the cave covert Tim saw them skirting the bank of the creek and swarming to a bridge that crossed it a few rods away. If only one or two of them would leap down and try to ford the stream—

But none of them did. Like a thick swarm of locusts, they clung close together and spread out on the other bank, to resume their dogged plodding to the south. Vainly Tim hoped for stragglers. There were none, for behind the waves of captives came the Japanese, to see that none lagged. Not until they had passed did Tim dare lead the way out of their shelter—to face eight discouraged, crestfallen men.

"That didn't work," he rallied them quickly, "but we aren't licked yet. They will probably be coming back, bringing new prisoners with them—and then we may have a better chance to fall on a small party and grab a few of them. If we can find some effective shelter—a farmhouse or a small village where they will be sure to pass—"

"Denham—less'n a mile ahead—and it's on the main road," Dawson supplied promptly. "It's so small the Japs'd never think of searching it a second time."

DENHAM PROVED to be a collection of no more than a dozen houses, a mere crossroads settlement that served the surrounding territory with a post office and three small stores.

Like everything in that blighted countryside, the buildings were deserted and locked up, but Tim forced the door of a large grain and feed depot on the northern edge of the village and led his party inside.

For half an hour they waited there, taking turns watching from the upper windows, before Dawson's keen eyes spotted the first sign of the returning column still far in the distance. Intently he peered through his glasses and frowned, shook his head dourly.

His words were gloomy.

"Don't look so good," he muttered. "They're coming back just about as close-packed as they went—maybe even more so. When they come along this road they're gonna be quite a crowd—"

And then the glasses almost dropped from his hands! Suddenly the crackle of shots had broken out very close to them—five or six reports, and then a terrific crash!

"The other side of the building!" Tim snapped, and led the way to the windows where the rest of his men were already clustering.

On the highway no more than fifty yards from the depot an armored car had collided with a truck and almost demolished it. In the ditch beside the wrecked truck Tim could see several people scrambling to their feet; could see them triggering shots at the car as its rear door opened and Japanese soldiers began to leap out. Frantically the figures in the ditch climbed out and started to run; two men and a woman—and suddenly Tim recognized them!

"Operator 5!" he gasped. "That's Operator 5—and Nan!"

The Japanese had followed for no more than ten yards. Now they were on their knees, taking careful aim for a volley that would be as deadly as the blast of an execution squad. But before Tim could say another word automatics blazed from every window on that side of the building. Out of it poured a hail of lead that hurled the Japanese back on their heels and dropped them almost where they stood.

With a wild yell of greeting, Tim led the way to the rescued trio and brought them back to the grain depot.

"That was mighty close," Tom Cahill mopped his brow after swift explanations had been completed, "but we're not out of this thing yet. That mob will be here in less than five minutes—" he eyed the oncoming horde of know-nothing men—"and if they happen to take a notion to look in here we're finished. I'm going out to have a look at that armored car," sudden inspiration came to him. "It may still be in running order."

When he had gone, the others resumed their watch, augmented by Jimmy and Nan Christopher—but now Tim Donovan had fresh cause for concern. Before that outburst of firing he had just about decided to chance everything this time and make a desperate effort to capture one of the know-nothing men by luring a few of them into the grain depot. Now that strategy was far too dangerous. As Tom Cahill had pointed out, if they were discovered they would be overwhelmed—and that would mean sure death for Operator 5 and Nan.

Worriedly he resumed his post at one of the upper windows and grimly watched the oncoming horde, his mind teeming with desperate plans that had to be rejected one after the other. All were too wild, too fraught with risk for the man whose life America could not afford to lose—all except one…. Tim's freckled face paled and his gray-blue eyes rounded as that plan dawned in his brain, but gradually they became steely hard and his jaw set with grim determination.

He had given his word to Norman King, and he would keep it….

Tensely all eleven of them crouched around the doors of the grain depot as the know-nothing men swarmed back along the road to the north. In a solid wave they came, a deep cordon that swept the fields as far as the watchers could see. But that wave had to part and flow around the buildings of the village. That jammed them up on the highway. Hundreds of them plodded stolidly along the road, but instinct seemed to keep them close together.

"There's no chance," Jimmy Christopher ruled. "Don't attempt anything, men. They will overwhelm us—and the Japs are coming along too closely behind them. Stay back from the doors."

Operator 5 was right, of course. Tim watched that close-packed horde trudge past—and the steel gleam in his eyes became even harder. Now the Japanese infantrymen were in the tiny village—but there were only a few of them; less than a score. Tim was just inside the main door of the building when the Japanese were almost abreast of it—and before his companions could stop him he suddenly yanked it open and lurched out into the middle of the road!

Like a drunken man he staggered into the highway, clutching at his throat and reeling dizzily—to drop to the ground almost in front of the surprised Orientals. For a moment they stopped and regarded him suspiciously. Then one of them laughed and stooped over him—to plunge the point of a hypodermic needle into his neck and discharge its contents....

That had all taken place so swiftly that the astounded watchers in the granary could not interfere until it was too late. Wide-eyed with horror, Operator 5 saw that syringe discharge its load of brain-paralyzing drug. His finger tightened on the trigger of his automatic—but he held it taut just as he was about to put a bullet through the head of the bending Jap. For suddenly he had realized Tim Donovan's incredible intention.

Tim was keeping his word to Doc King! He had staggered out there deliberately, to give King a know-nothing man for his experiments!

Now he was staggering to his feet, his face already blank and expressionless as the Japs took him by the arms and turned him toward the north. One of them pointed, and Tim started plodding forward docilely, his will power already subjugated and destroyed.

Cold prickles ran up and down Jimmy Christopher's spine as he watched that uncanny transformation—and then he snapped out of the near-coma that horror had plunged him into.

"Let them have it!" he rasped—and a withering fire poured into the amazed Japanese.

Even before that party of infantrymen was wiped out, Jimmy sprang into the roadway and ran to intercept Tim. Again chill horror gripped him as he peered into the gray-blue eyes and found them utterly without expression, as cold and blank as the eyes of a fish. Tim looked at him and did not know him, did not even seem to see him; kept right on walking toward the north, like a mechanical toy that has been wound up and set in motion.

"All right, Tim, boy," Jimmy tried to soothe him and put an arm around his shoulder. "We'll take care of you. We're all ready to start back now, Tim. We'll take you to Doc King—"

But Tim Donovan threw off the encircling arm without a word, cast it from him with strength that amazed Jimmy. Straight ahead he plodded—until Jimmy blocked his way and seized him, to hold him back forcibly; and even then, it was more than a one-man job to turn him from his course. Ed Garland came to his rescue, and between them they lifted Tim bodily and started to carry him despite his struggles.

"Watch yourselves! Here they come!" old Dawson shouted a warning at that moment; and suddenly the village seemed to be full of Japanese.

THE SOUND of firing had brought the Japs from every direction. Barely in time Jimmy and Garland got their struggling burden back into the granary. Bullets were whistling around their heads as they ducked through the door and slammed it tight behind them.

Once he was in the building, out of sight of the road which he had been commanded to follow, Tim Donovan's mania left him. Meekly he sank down on a bag of grain, a spiritless, mindless thing who could only wait to be told what to do....

Jimmy Christopher's heart ached at that sight, but now there was no time for pity. There were at least fifty Japanese outside the building, and others were arriving steadily. Despite the fire from the defenders, the Orientals were pounding on the doors, and Jimmy knew that it would be only a matter of minutes before they would be inside.

Tom Cahill—how had he made out with that armored car?

Old Dawson answered that question as he came down from where he had been with several of the men at an upper window.

"Your man's got that car a-going," he reported. "He's coming up here with it now—but getting aboard's going to be something of a problem. We've sorta figured, Operator 5, that the most important cargo is the lady here and this young feller—and yourself. You're getting in while—"

"No, you don't—" Jimmy started to protest, as an outbreak of excited yelling in front of the building told him that the armored car must have arrived. But suddenly Ed Garland leaped upon him and held him fast.

At the same moment the big front door of the granary was thrown wide—and out rushed seven men with blazing guns. The surprise of their sudden charge swept the Japanese back and gave Tom Cahill a chance to open the car's rear door. Mitchell and one of the Shepards were down by now, but the other five clustered around that door, a human screen, while Nan climbed inside. Gilman and Sharp crumpled beneath the Japanese fire before Tim could be pushed in after her. Johnson slumped in a heap and the second Shepard pitched forward on his face as Jimmy fairly hurled Ed Garland in—but before he could force old Dawson to follow, he was pushed in himself and the door slammed shut.

The old man was down on his knees, but his guns accounted for three more of the Japs who came running toward the car with grenades; held the rest back until Cahill could throw the engine into gear and speed out onto the corpse-littered road. For just a moment Dawson reared to his feet—and suddenly he seemed disintegrate, blown into atoms!

"A grenade," Jimmy Christopher answered Nan's unspoken question. "He threw himself in the way and caught it—or it would have blown this car into little pieces."

"They don't make them any braver than old Dawson," Ed Garland said huskily—and his eyes turned to where Tim Donovan sat, dull and vacant-eyed, staring in front of him without the slightest understanding. "Or Tim Donovan," he amended softly.

Tim's little squad of volunteers had been sadly depleted, but they had accomplished what they had set out to do. That Japanese armored car, rushing back to the American lines, was carrying the drug-infected specimen Norman King needed so badly; the know-nothing man Tim Donovan had promised to bring him!

CHAPTER 8
AMERICA UNDER THE VULTURE'S SHADOW

TIM DONOVAN would have to be rushed to Washington, where he would receive the best of care and where the scientists of the War Department Research Laboratory could study him and conduct their experiments. Norman King decided that the moment he saw the "captive" Tim had brought him. Nan Christopher went along with them, to assist Dr. King in his vital work.

Operator 5 saw them to the plane, and turned away with a heavy heart. Part of himself was going to Washington with that stricken lad, and he dearly would have loved to have gone along—but, at a time as crucial as he now faced, he could not leave his post.

For him there waited days of worry and toil, days of maddening retreat while he marshaled every resource of the nation in a desperate effort to stem the Japanese advance. That grim battle was not without victories; and he at least had the satisfaction of knowing that he was throwing Hachibu Aiko's carefully mapped out program far behind schedule. Yet the devastating blot of Japanese invasion kept spreading irresistibly. He had to watch it cover Nebraska and Kansas, Minnesota, Iowa and Missouri; and then begin to creep so terribly into Wisconsin and Illinois.

Hour after hour, Operator 5 conferred with the defense chiefs, mapping new lines that always crumbled, planning new strategy that seemed always doomed to failure. Again and again he went back to the map and stared down at the sorry story of a nation that was in its death throes.

The Atlantic coast from Maine to the District of Columbia, and nearly as far west as Buffalo, was still a devastated ruin, the work of Kasuga-Tosa and his fire-belching rocket-planes.* The harried inhabitants who had fled from death in this area and sought refuge in the Mid-West had now turned, like badgered sheep, and were fleeing from an even worse fate that confronted them where they had thought to find peace and security. They were filtering back into New York and New England, beginning the task of rebuilding the fire-gutted cities Kasuga-Tosa had left in his wake. But it would take months, even years, before this work would have progressed to the point where the nation could look to that fire-scarred region for aid.

The American army, badly shattered and demoralized by the grueling campaign against Kasuga-Tosa, had retreated to the Appalachians, where General Hugh Thayer, the new commander-in-chief, now was making a herculean effort to reorganize it and move westward to meet the new menace. But that, too, would take time.

"Time—time!" Operator 5 groaned. "If we only had time, America could meet and defeat any onslaught the Japanese might devise. But they are here, right in our midst, without warning; and every passing hour means the loss of thousands of lives and the spread of the panic that threatens to undermine and ruin us!"

Until the national army could come to the rescue, militia units were holding the battle line on the east and the south—

* AUTHOR'S NOTE: For an account of the sudden and mystifying doom with which Rai Kasuga-Tosa confronted America and of Operator 5's defense against it, the reader is referred to "Invasion from the Sky."

and, Jimmy could only hope, on the west. Fighting desperately to keep the enemy away from the vital manufacturing cities of the East, he did not dare leave that front long enough to make a trip to the West but had to depend upon often-interrupted wire and badly scrambled radio communications with the defense headquarters on the Wyoming-Colorado battlefront.

Vainly Operator 5 hurled the nation's best aircraft against the invaders—until he was convinced that it was murder to send flyers against ships many times larger and more powerful than their own. The American planes were no match for these leviathans of the enemy, which continued to fly in reinforcements and fresh supplies across the Canadian border. Instead of diminishing, the Japanese force, thus fed, continued to grow steadily; and the shocktroops they made of their American captives mounted by leaps and bounds, despite the fact that most of the area in the path of the air-armada was being evacuated by all but its desperate defenders.

Hachibu Aiko had grown wily since he had found that the terror of his approach depopulated the country before his planes reached it. Instead of following his methodical plan and pushing forward his advance a regular distance each day, he was sending his ships on surprise forays, leaping far ahead at one point and then at another, so that the blot on the map was no longer round and smooth-edged but began to resemble an ugly splash. By the thousands these tactics added to his helpless native cohorts.

By the end of a week after Tim Donovan's martyrdom General Thayer's rejuvenated troops began to move westward and the army engineers set them to work constructing a new line which the Japanese must not be allowed to pass. Once that line crumbled, Chicago, and after that all the industrial cities beyond it that were the very heart-beat of the nation, would be at the mercy of the triumphant invaders.

"We can build a line that will hold, a line that they will never pass," Thayer spoke for his engineers, "but we have to have time, Operator 5. Our men are working twenty-four hours a day, but we can't perform miracles. We ought to have months for preparation, but we will do it in weeks—if you can give us the weeks."

"You will have them, General," Jimmy promised—and then began a defense campaign such as the world had never seen. OVER THOUSANDS of square miles, the length and breadth of Wisconsin and Illinois, Operator 5 traveled; and wherever he went he sounded the clear call of patriotism—the call of sacrifice, to death!

"We cannot defend this territory," he told the inhabitants frankly. "It will be overrun during the next week or two—but I want to hold it until the very last moment. Every hour counts. I want men who will stay here until the bitter end—who are willing to die here in order to save America from destruction."

Over and over he repeated that challenge; in isolated homes, in country stores, at town meetings, in motion picture theaters, on the corners of city streets. And by the dozens, the scores, the hundreds, volunteers flocked to his banner and were assigned to their tasks. All through that territory that would soon fall into the hands of the Japanese he posted sharpshooters who knew that sure death would be their lot—and who accepted it grimly, defiantly.

"Avoid the *American* captives, the know-nothing men," he instructed them. "Let them pass. It is the Japanese we want. You will be provided with a gas mask that will get you through the barrage of darkness and an automatic rifle. You will be posted where you can do the most harm. The Japanese will get you—but it will be up to you how dearly they have to pay for ousting you from your vantage-point."

Not only did he fill the countryside with sharpshooters ready to snipe at the Orientals from every possible covert, but Operator 5 studded their way with traps that took a deadly toll for every mile of American territory they covered. In stores and gas stations, in farmhouses and city homes, in culverts and in city sewers, he posted men whose duty it was to stay there until the Japanese were on top of them—and then set off the explosion that would mean death for themselves as well as the enemy.

"That's soldiering for old men," one old graybeard spoke up when Jimmy stopped to make his appeal in a little town on the edge of Madison. "I was born here, and I intend to die here—so I reckon I might as well do some good while I'm a-doin' it. We have a club of us old fellers here—veterans of the Purple Wars. We'll take care of this for you, Operator 5—and we'll show these smart army muckamucks that we can soldier just as well as these youngsters they put in uniforms!"

The spirit of America—regardless of age! Martyrs all, they wrote a glorious page in American history!

The Japanese came on, behind their planes and their gas barrage, behind their waves of helpless captives; but they died by the hundreds, by the thousands. They swept everything before them, but, like the British going back to Boston from Concord in 1775, death harried them from every possible sniping post. Like the Minute Men who fought from behind every stone wall, these patriots of two centuries later contested every foot of the way, their only hope to inflict as much damage as possible and to gain a few precious hours for Operator 5 and the sweating thousands who were toiling to complete the new defense line miles behind them.

Thousands worked day and night on that long line of entrenchments, but they were not the only ones Operator 5 marshaled in this national crisis. Throughout the East, in city after city, mills and factories responded to his appeal by working at top speed. Millions labored as they never had worked before, toiling to produce the armament so desperately needed, to provide the men at the front with munitions and modern weapons that would be the equal of those they must face.

And still a third army worked ceaselessly, unsleeping—a little army whose members Operator 5 met individually as he went from city to city. Members of his nationwide undercover organization, whose duty it was to see to it that the labor of these workers was not betrayed by sabotage.

Those men died, too—many of them. Their deaths were not chronicled in the newspapers; they were buried without trumpets and fanfare—only their fellows knew of their passing.

"Thompson was killed Tuesday night—run over by an automobile.... Perry's body was found yesterday morning in the river.... There was an accident at the plant; Ricker was killed when a crane dropped a beam on his head.... Hosie died in the hospital this morning—poisoned food."

One by one, those disguised reports came to Operator 5—and for each he added another gold star to that Roll of Honor.

Back, back, steadily back, fighting grimly for every mile—it seemed that that death-studded retreat never would end. But at last it was over. At last the new defense line was completed—a line that was equipped with the very latest of aircraft defense; that was fortified with high-powered guns and deadly ray-projectors; that boasted signal apparatus which detected the Japanese aerial advance from afar and enabled the anti-aircraft men to put up a barrage that was impassable.

At long last the Japanese advance was stopped, along a great line that ran from the Great Lakes to Tennessee; a line that ran about sixty miles west of Green Bay, Sheboygan, Racine and Chicago and then swung westward to protected Memphis in the south. At last there was a breathing spell—and Operator 5 promptly prepared to take the offensive. From Memphis to Chicago he patrolled that line—and then continued on by plane to Canada to try to win reinforcements for the hard-pressed American troops.

"OUR CAUSE is one, as it always has been, Operator 5," Sir John Bacon, the Canadian Governor-General, assured him warmly at the close of that historic meeting. "The resources of the Dominion—such as they are—are yours to command. We were not able to recuperate as quickly as the United States from the destruction wrought by the armies of the Purple Empire. As you know, much of our Western provinces has sunk back to the status of a wilderness, which is why the Japanese have been able to land and establish a base there unopposed. But we will fight shoulder to shoulder with you in your defense line to oust them now that they are here. I shall send out a call for volunteers today and rush help to you as quickly as we can possibly manage it."

With that welcome promise of reinforcements ringing in his ears, Operator 5 flew back to the United States and landed at headquarters behind the new defense line—only to find, to his amazement, that a strange change had taken place during his three-day absence.

He noticed it immediately in the usually cordial men at the landing field, in the troops he passed on his way to the headquarters building, even in the officers he greeted—they all looked at him queerly. Some appeared to be suspicious of him, some hostile, some contemptuous—and still others pitying! Something was wrong—very, very wrong; and he intended to find out what it was promptly....

That did not take him long. The moment he stepped into General Thayer's quarters, he read the troubled look in his friend's eyes.

"What is all this, General?" he snapped. "Something is the matter. Let me have it straight."

"I don't know how to say it, Operator 5," Thayer stammered. "I hate to have to be the one to tell you—but, at that, it is probably better that you have it from me than from one of the others. But first, tell me—where have you been since you left Chicago?"

"Ottawa—and then to a retreat of Sir John Bacon's in the Laurentian Hills, north of Montreal," Jimmy told him.

"I need not have asked, of course," Thayer apologized, "but there is another report here. They say you were in Washington—that you conspired with Vice President Tobey and headed a revolution that ousted Andrew Warren and put Tobey in his place."

Revolution! Andrew Warren ousted from the Presidency! Jimmy could hardly believe what he had heard.

"What has happened to Andy Warren, Thayer—tell me, is he all right?" he demanded anxiously.

"So far as we know, he is in prison," Thayer answered. "Telegraphic communication with the capital has been cut off for the past two days, but two officers, members of the general staff, arrived by plane last night and brought the news. It spread like wildfire, and in some unaccountable fashion it reached the troops."

"And I am thoroughly discredited, is that it?" Operator 5's face was white and set, his jaw square and hard, and his eyes blazed—with the light of battle!

"At any other time, such a report would receive no more serious attention than it deserves," Thayer tried to make the blow easier; "but, at a time like this, with everyone's nerves on edge—you can understand what the reaction would be. Needless to say, Operator 5, your friends are standing by you—but, frankly, we do not know where to turn."

"The army is loyal to the President?" Jimmy snapped.

"Of course."

"Good. Now, where are these officers from the capital?" was

Jimmy's next question. "I am much interested in what they have to say."

"That will be easy." Thayer glanced at his watch. "We are having a staff meeting in about ten minutes. They will both be there."

Major John Rein and Captain Theodore Clarey were both in their seats when Operator 5 entered the staff meeting with General Thayer. Rein he had met several times in Washington; Clarey was a stranger to him—but they both regarded him with angry, hostile eyes—and they were not acting. Jimmy studied them keenly and was almost certain of that; their indignation was too genuine, their aversion too patent. Something had happened down there in Washington that had affected them profoundly—but *what?*

At General Thayer's request, Major Rein repeated his story.

"The government is now in the hands of Clarman Tobey, who has declared himself President—backed up by Operator 5!" he flung his challenge at Jimmy as he finished.

"As I told you last evening, Major Rein," Thayer answered him, "there must be some mistake about this. Operator 5 has just returned from Canada, where he has been in conference with the Governor-General."

"He has just returned from Washington!" Rein flared hotly. "Captain Cleary and I both saw him there—and he knows it!"

Pandemonium reigned in the room after that. A dozen officers were on their feet at once, all shouting and trying to make themselves heard. Operator 5's friends sprang to his defense indignantly, but Rein and Clarey were not without their partisans—and Jimmy noticed that there were others who sat back doubtfully and tried to decide what to believe. Their confidence in him was not easily shaken—and yet these officers did not have the appearance of malicious liars....

"There seems to be one way of settling this, gentlemen," Jimmy addressed them, when quiet was restored. "I am going to Washington to confront Clarman Tobey—and I invite Major Rein and Captain Clarey to accompany me, as representatives of this staff and the whole army." That suggestion was acceptable to everybody, and Jimmy made immediate arrangements for his departure—but before the plane was ready he saw and heard plenty to deepen the lines of worry in his brow. No matter what their intention might have been, Major Rein and Captain Clarey had done almost irreparable harm with their announcement. These panicky, half-demoralized troops had believed in Operator 5 as they believed in nobody else—and now their faith was undermined and shaken.

What might happen there before he returned, he did not like to think. And when would he return? What would he find awaiting him when he alighted in Washington? Those questions and worries throbbed through his brain as he stepped into the army bomber with the two officers—and realized that he was virtually a prisoner, under arrest until he was able to prove his innocence....

CHAPTER 9
DEATH FOR PATRIOTS!

T HAT JOURNEY to Washington was one of maddening suspense. Hour after hour, Operator 5 struggled to make head or tail of the amazing situation; tried to arrive at some approximation of what could have transpired in the capital in those crucial hours when the nation's very life hung precariously in the balance.

Clarman Tobey, he knew, was a weakling. At the height of the terror created by Kasuga-Tosa's depredations, he had tried to surrender abjectly to the Japanese the moment control of the government temporarily fell into his hands. Operator 5 had forcibly thwarted that cowardly attempt—and had earned Clarman Tobey's undying hatred by doing so.

Was it possible that now, trembling in fear of the on-coming Japanese air-armada, the man might have become desperate—so desperate that he had taken the situation into his own hands? Andrew Warren never would have listened to a suggestion of yielding. Was it possible that Tobey had received one of Moto Taronago's threats and had been stampeded into overthrowing and imprisoning Warren so that he could seize the Presidency himself and make terms with the invaders?

Operator 5's teeth gritted and his nails dug deep into the palms of his hands at that humiliating thought!

But this purported backing by Operator 5—that was altogether incomprehensible…. Unless Tobey had been taken in by the same masquerader who had posed as Operator 5 in Los

Angeles…. Even a panic-stricken Tobey should have known better than that…. Which left only one answer—that Clarman Tobey was knowingly using this pretender, this creature of the Yellow Vulture's, for his own ends; was knowingly playing hand in glove with the man whose Asiatic horde was overrunning the heart of America….

Jimmy's endless speculations tormented him until the wheels of the big bomber came down on the turf of Sheridan airport. Then they were thrust aside for firsthand observation. Washington may have been torn with revolution, but he noticed no evidence of it there at the field. Everything seemed to be going on as usual—except for the sidelong glances he caught from those he passed; enigmatic glances that were divided between subservience and contempt.

Washington evidently was divided in its opinion of this new role of Operator 5's, he told himself grimly. Some, the toadyers, were quick to bend the knee to the new power that ruled their destinies. But others, real Americans who had no use for treachery and double-crossing, recognized this erstwhile champion of theirs for what he now stood revealed to be—a god with feet of shoddy clay….

"We will go to my office first, gentlemen," he requested, as Rein and Oarey stepped out of the plane.

The officers nodded acquiescence and stepped into a cab with him. Their attitude throughout the journey had interested him greatly, and now he covertly studied them. At first they were openly hostile and contemptuous. But as the hours passed and something of that indefinable charm—that rare personal magnetism—that was Operator 5's reached out and enveloped them, they began to mellow, to become more civil. Now regret was clearly evident in their faces as they squared their shoulders and prepared to do their duty.

Since this amazing charge had been leveled at him, Jimmy Christopher had felt as if he moved in a strange, unreal world. But the moment he stepped into the hallway of the building that housed his office he was on familiar ground. Upstairs his father would be on duty; would no doubt be worrying himself sick over his inability to reach Jimmy. He would know exactly what had happened.

John Christopher was sitting at the big desk in the inner office when Jimmy strode into it, but his face was haggard and deathly pale. His eyes flashed a warning and he tried to speak. But before the words could leave his lips men appeared from everywhere—from the side offices, from the closets, from the hallway behind Jimmy. Men with guns who crowded around Operator 5 and the two officers, disarmed them.

"You are under arrest, Operator 5—you and these staff officers who have been absent from Washington without leave," a big man who seemed to be their leader announced.

"On whose authority? On what charge? Who *are* you?" Jimmy's questions barked at the fellow.

"On the authority of the President of the United States, Clarman Tobey; on the charges of conspiracy and treason," the big man answered. "I am Morgan Parker, of the reorganized Secret Service."

"I tried to reach you, Jimmy," John Christopher quavered. "I have been helpless here, a prisoner—while they took charge of the office—"

Before he was finished, they bustled Jimmy and the two officers out and downstairs to where two cars awaited them. But grim exultation leaped in Jimmy's heart as he went. He had seen the surprise in the eyes of Rein and Clarey. Now at least they realized their mistake—which meant that his vindication had begun!

THE CARS drove across Washington and stopped at a four-story residential building that was on the block beyond the Senate office building. He noted this as they were ordered out and hurried to the entrance. A man answered the door when his captors rang, but otherwise the building seemed to be silent and unoccupied—what he saw of it. That was very little, for he was led through the hallway and down a stairs to the basement, then down another stairs into a dimly lit sub-cellar from which a long tunnel corridor seemed to delve into the bowels of the earth.

This finally terminated in a huge, musty vault, the walls of which were pocked with tiny cubicles of cells. Into one of these Jimmy was thrust. The metal door, solid except for a foot-square, barred opening near the top, was closed and locked after him; and then he heard doors clanging shut on Major Rein and Captain Clarey.

So this was Clarman Tobey's private jail, somewhere deep under the streets of Washington—where Jimmy was as securely immured as if he were in his grave. With an impostor at large in the capital to take his place, John Christopher was the only one who would have any inkling of what had happened to him—and undoubtedly his lips would be promptly and effectively sealed.

Somewhere under the streets of Washington…. The silence of the tomb settled over the place when Tobey's secret police had gone—silence that was broken at intervals by a low rumbling. The noise of a streetcar overhead, probably, Jimmy told himself, and vainly tried to figure where that long subterranean corridor could have taken them.

"I want to apologize, Operator 5—not that apologies are worth much now," John Rein's voice interrupted his thoughts. "We've been fooled nicely, Clarey and I—though I'll be damned if I know how they put it over. I would have been willing to bet my life that I saw you here in Washington with Clarman Tobey."

"Operator 5?" another voice came from across the wide vault. "Jimmy—have they got you here, too?"

The voice of the President! Andrew Warren was imprisoned in that underground jail also!

The despair in Warren's voice touched Jimmy to the quick, but what could he do to ease it? What hope could he offer now? He answered quickly, and in a few moments Andrew Warren was pouring out his troubles; relating what little he knew about his overthrow.

"I went to the President's room in the Senate wing of the Capitol," he recounted wearily. "There were some bills awaiting my signature. Clarman Tobey spread them on the desk before me—and then someone clapped a chloroform-soaked cloth over my face. That is the last I remember—seeing Tobey looking down at me with a satisfied smile as my senses left me. When I woke up I was here."

And God only knew how much longer he would be there, Jimmy admitted to himself, as he paced his narrow cell and realized what little chance he had of escaping from it. The place was impregnable, escape-proof without aid from the outside— and what chance was there for outside aid here deep under the surface of the ground?

The jailer was the only possibility. But when he arrived, some hours later, that slight hope vanished also. He was an elderly man, gray-haired and stoop-shouldered, mild-faced—and he held up a warning hand as soon as he entered the cell with a tray of food.

"Don't try to jump me, Operator 5; it won't do you any good," he warned. "I ain't got a gun. You can knock me out, but you'd never get out of this place. There's guards at the door all the time, especially when they know I'm in here. I ain't got nothing against you, Operator 5," he tried to be friendly, conciliatory. "I'm Jason. You don't remember me, of course, but I fought under you at the Battle of Hoboken. That's where I got *this*." He shrugged his left shoulder which was higher than his right. "I ain't got nothing against you—I just got my job to 'tend to here."

"I understand, Jason," Jimmy nodded—but his pulses leaped with excitement, for his quick eyes had noticed something that promised at least a faint ray of hope....

Here was an idea!

After the jailer had gone, he pondered that discovery for a long while. Then he took a notebook from his pocket and opened it to a clean page. From inside the lining of his coat came a little pellet which he dissolved in a quantity of his drinking water, and a small, split quill which would serve as a pen. Dipping it into the water, he wrote a carefully worded note that gave the address of the house to which he had been taken—a note which disappeared the moment the water dried. The rest of his plan would have to wait until morning, when Jason would come with breakfast....

OPERATOR 5 mustered every iota of his dramatic ability for that all-important moment. The old man had come into his cell and was setting down the breakfast tray, when Jimmy drew back from him in wide-eyed alarm. Surprised, Jason looked down at himself; looked at his left hand and wrist, where a deep cut had been allowed to go unattended until it had become infected. The hand was swollen, and the edges of the wound were a nasty purple, with angry red blotches running up past his wrist.

"Oh, that," he muttered. "I done that last week. Cut it on a piece of tin—and it don't seem to get much better."

"Better?" Jimmy's voice was low and shocked, the voice of one who speaks to a man he knows is doomed. "How do you expect it to get better? It's infected!" Gingerly he lifted the old man's hand and looked at it carefully. "Just as I thought," he nodded his head deploringly, "the poison has entered your veins. I'm surprised that you are able to stand on your feet, Jason. You don't feel sleepy, do you?"

"N-no...." Jason was uncertain.

"That's lucky for you," Jimmy congratulated him. "If you feel that sleepiness coming on, it means that the poison has reached your heart. You just drowse off—and you never wake up. I'm surprised it hasn't hit you already, such a hand!"

"What'll I do for it?" Old Jason was trembling now and his face was turning a sickly green. "Maybe I better go see a doctor—huh?"

"Most doctors will not be able to help you now—the poison has gone too far." Jimmy looked dubious. "There is one who might, though—he will be able to if any man can," he brightened suddenly. "Doctor King, over at the War Department Laboratory—do you know him? I'll give you a note to him, and the visit won't cost you anything."

Out of his pocket he took the notebook, turned to the page on which he had worked the night before, and wrote a brief note with his fountain-pen, asking King to give Jason immediate treatment before his infection proved fatal. Tearing the page from the notebook, he held it out to the old man. But Jason regarded it dubiously, his fright battling with his sense of duty.

"There is nothing there to get you into trouble. Read it yourself," Jimmy snapped, and now there was a hint of mastery in his voice, the tone that men obeyed. "You need not tell the doctor where I am or anything about me, if he should ask. But if you want to keep on tending these cells, you had better not waste any time before you get over to see him. How soon can you go there?"

"Well, I dunno—maybe just before lunch. I can get off then—and it oughtn't to take me long."

The note was folded up and in his pocket when Jason left the cell, and Operator 5 sat back to hope as he never had hoped before. Would Jason go to Norman King? Would King understand and heat the paper so that the invisible-ink message would be legible? Would he be able to summon help and penetrate to this underground jail?

QUESTIONS... THEY ran through Jimmy's brain endlessly, while the passing minutes became hours. Eleven-thirty, twelve, twelve-thirty; and Jason came in with another tray of food. The first thing that Jimmy saw was the bandage on the old man's arm—and his heart leaped.

"I been there," Jason confided. "He's a nice feller, that doctor. He read your note and looked at my hand, and he said he realized the seriousness of the situation. He put some kind of salve on it that made it feel a lot better—sorta soothing, it is."

Norman King realized the seriousness of the situation! He had understood; had read the hidden message. And now he would go into action, losing no time in reaching those loyal friends who still could be counted upon to stand by Operator 5! But how soon would he be able to accomplish anything? How soon would he be able to bring help? Probably not for a day or more, at best....

But Norman King worked much more swiftly than that....

The hours seemed to drag endlessly, but it was no more than two-thirty when Jimmy heard a commotion in the corridor that led to the subterranean vault. Footsteps and the sound of excited, angry voices. He went to the barred window of his cell and saw the vault door open; saw three men stride in with Jason, and recognized the leader as Morgan Parker, the big fellow who had been in charge of the men who had arrested him.

Parker's face was twisted with rage as he strode to Jimmy's cell and peered through the bars.

"I don't know how you pulled it, wise guy," he snarled. "I don't know how you tipped off your gang where we took you, but it won't get you anywhere—don't forget that. There's a mob of a thousand or so of your admirers upstairs trying to find you, but they won't get anywhere even if they pull the house down. This part down here has already been shut off so that nobody in the world could find it. They're just doing a lot of hollering and yelling for nothing.

"Meanwhile—" he turned to where Jason was opening Andrew Warren's cell—"we're going to take you out of here, Mr. Ex-President. If that crowd gets out of hand maybe you will want to have a few words to say to them to prevent their getting hurt."

Between them they marched Warren out of the vault, and again silence settled over the place. But now Jimmy could hardly restrain himself from trying to tear down the walls with his bare hands. Norman King had done more than bring help. He must have appealed to the crowd, must have raised the populace, with whom Operator 5 still was a national hero—and now they were storming the house, threatening to tear it down in order to rescue him! And he had to sit there, helpless, impotent, while his friends did battle for him....

Glumly he slumped on the edge of his cot, and again that low rumble sounded in his ears. A street-car? But there *were* no street-cars in that section of Washington. If not a street-car, what could be causing this peculiar noise?

Suddenly Jimmy straightened like a ramrod. He *knew!* And now he knew why Morgan Parker was not more concerned about the crowd breaking into the residential building into which the captive had been taken. They were no longer in that building—they were somewhere in the cellars of the big Senate office building!

Somehow he must get out of that cell! Somehow he must get to that crowd of would-be rescuers and lead them to Andrew Warren before they became discouraged and turned away! But how? *How?*

The answer came unexpectedly—not more than ten minutes after Andrew Warren had been taken from the vault. Again the door from the corridor opened, and old Jason came in. He seemed listless and his feet shuffled tiredly, Jimmy noted. The old fellow approached his cell, unlocked the door to take away the lunch tray. Groggily, he stepped inside and slumped on the cot.

"It's come—like you said, Operator 5," he husked. "I guess I got to the doctor too late. I'm getting sleepy—so tired I can hardly keep my eyes open. I'm gonna fall asleep—and I won't wake up no more. But I hadda come in to see you first—before I die. This shoulder—they'd have killed me that day if it hadn't been for you. You come charging in and saved me, and I been keeping you locked up here. But now—now you can go. I don't care what… they do to me…."

The old man's eyes were nearly closed; he could barely hold up his head. Drugged, undoubtedly—and in that moment Operator 5 gave fervent thanks for Norman King. King was the answer; he must have bound Jason's open sore with a narcotic

140

dressing that had gradually worked its way into his blood! King had gambled that the sleepiness of the jailer might give Jimmy the chance he needed to escape!

"Thanks, Jason," Jimmy said softly, as he took the keys from the old man's belt. "I'll get the doctor and see what we can do for you."

Swiftly he stepped out of his cell and ran to the one in which Major Rein was confined, then to Captain Clarey's. They were free now, but there still remained the guards outside the door to pass. Armed with nothing but the light trays that had held their lunch, they approached the corridor door—and suddenly it was flung wide. In the doorway, with drawn guns leveled, stood Morgan Parker and two of the guards.

JOHN REIN was half a step in advance at that moment—and before anyone could anticipate his intention he flung himself forward. Like Arnold van Winkelreed on the blood-soaked Swiss battlefield, he flung himself forward with wide-spread arms that closed on the weapons of his enemies. All three of those guns he wrapped in his embrace—and all three of them poured their deadly lead into his body!

Rein went down, but even before he hit the floor Operator 5 and Theodore Clarey were leaping over his falling body, their fists smashing savagely into the faces of the guards. Caught tight in Rein's death-grip, the men were momentarily helpless. One staggered backward and dropped like a pole-axed steer when Jimmy's fist caught him under the jaw. Another rocked groggily on his feet as Clarey flailed away at him. And then Jimmy had his fingers on the gun that his man had dropped. Half-way up from the floor, he fired—and Morgan Parker pitched forward with a hole drilled between his eyes as the bullet from his own weapon singed Jimmy's neck!

Back along the tunnel corridor Operator 5 led the way, and then off into an alcove that he had noticed as he passed. At one side of that little station was a doorway—and a stairs that led to the floor above. The moment he reached that upper floor Jimmy knew that his hunch had been correct. Now he knew where he was—and where he must go.

"This is the Senate office building," he called to Clarey. "The senators' private subway to the Capitol is just around that next corner. That's the noise we heard downstairs. That's where they took Warren—to the Capitol!"

Then they were around the turn, had commandeered one of the little cross-seated cars and forced the astonished operator to get it going. The moment it stopped beneath the Capitol, they leaped out; and again Jimmy led the way—for now he knew just where he was going.

Andrew Warren had said that the last thing he could remember the day he was abducted was that he was in the President's room of the Senate wing—and it was from there that he had been taken down to the underground railway. The President's room was used only by him and by newspapermen when Congress was in session. A place where his abductors would be quite safe from interruption....

Warily Operator 5 approached the door of that room, with Theodore Clarey close at his heels, but before they could reach it they knew that they were too late. Suddenly there was a commotion behind the door—chairs overturning, scrambling feet, men calling excited directions.

They had been warned—probably by the driver of the subway car!

Operator 5 was in the lead as he and Clarey charged. Crouching low, they vaulted through the door. But the room seemed empty of all except Andrew Warren, who sat at his big, flat-topped desk with a pen in his hand. White-faced and open-mouthed, he sat there and stared—and just in time Operator 5 flung himself to one side. The bullet that would have ended his life cut through the shoulder of his coat and gashed his back.

Now he was on his feet—face to face with *himself!* Face to face with a man so much like himself that they might have been identical twins! And in the same fraction of a second they were no longer so identical—for Operator 5's gun had spoken, and there was a bullet through the chest and another through the face of the man who had played his dangerous masquerade once too often.

Before the fellow's body hit the floor Jimmy was beside him, catching him and lowering him gently—and again he was amazed by that startling resemblance. No wonder that Rein and Clarey had been deceived; anyone might have been taken in by that impersonation. Perhaps even Clarman Tobey....

The fellow was trying to talk as Jimmy knelt above him, but blood was filling his mouth and drowning his words.

"Tobey—" he managed to gasp. "Tobey and Taronago—"

But what he intended to reveal was never permitted to leave his lips, for at that moment a gun crashed from the doorway

leading to the Senate chamber and a bullet tore through the dying man's skull. For a fraction of a second the hate-twisted face of Clarman Tobey was framed in the doorway. But even as Operator 5 triggered bullets through the panels the door slammed shut and a key turned.

BY THE time Jimmy made his way through another corridor Tobey had escaped from the building and it was afterwards learned, was on his way to a private plane usually kept in readiness for him on the edge of the city. He fled, and the trumped-up administration he had tried to set up collapsed with his flight. In a few hours the last of his henchmen who had not disappeared were under arrest, and the first illegal Presidency in American history was at an end....

"Thank God, you came when you did, Jimmy," Andrew Warren said fervently, as he tore up the paper which had been lying on the desk in front of him. "I do not believe I would have had very much longer to live unless I had signed the resignation they were trying to force upon me—and that, of course, I never would have done."

With President Warren restored to the White House, Operator 5 turned his attention to plans for storming and recapturing the Japanese-held territory. Long into that night he conferred with the general staff. At last every angle of the situation had been considered and the meeting was breaking up. Then there came a telephone call for Operator 5!

"General Thayer calling from eastern defense headquarters," the operator announced, and now the general's anxious voice came over the wire.

"Thank God, you have reopened telephone communication with the capital, Operator 5!" he exclaimed. "I have been trying all day to reach you. I don't know what you found in Washington—but a few hours after you left here the Japanese launched a drive that was irresistible. They shattered our line on a front nearly fifty miles long, from the Wisconsin-Illinois border south. We are striving desperately to reorganize, but I am afraid that tomorrow will be even worse than today."

Tomorrow Operator 5 would be there—but by then it might be too late. Back into his mind flashed the dying words of the man who had impersonated him, *"Tobey and Taronago."*

That was the answer; that was the devilish coupling that was responsible for this fresh debacle! The trick had been perfectly timed: to weaken the defense line by undermining the morale of the men and then to draw Operator 5 away from it when the drive was launched that would carry the Japanese finally on to take Chicago!

CHAPTER 10
THE AMERICAN SPIRIT

DIANE ELLIOT and General Thayer had walked to the plane with Operator 5 and the two officers who were to accompany him to Washington. When it had taken to the air and was no more than a black spot fading in the distance, they turned away, and neither of them spoke. There was too much to think about at that moment for words.

To Diane the whole thing had been incredible. She never

would have believed that men who had fairly idolized Operator 5 could suddenly turn against him—and yet she saw evidence of it on every side. Where she had been accustomed to nothing but smiles and polite salutes, she now met dark looks and faces that were seemingly accidentally turned away as she passed.

They were blind, stupid—poor misguided fools! But how could she hope to make them see that? She couldn't. General Thayer tried, in his way, and met with little success. He spoke to his officers and sternly forbade any further discussion of Operator 5, and then he spoke to the men; tried to pep them up and take their minds off the subject that he knew was being debated in every trench and dugout. But he could not drive the suspicion from their minds, nor restore that blind and implicit faith in Operator 5 that had often moved them to accomplish the seemingly impossible.

Some of them were bitter, hostile—contemptuous of Thayer's efforts to win them over. Others obviously wanted to be convinced. But the cancer of suspicion had eaten deep and could not lightly be eradicated.

Operator 5's friends—and there still were hundreds of them to every mile of that battle-front—tried in their own way to remedy the situation. But it only led to hot arguments and furious fights. More than once that morning Diane turned her eyes from a riotous free-for-all and tried not to realize that the good name of Operator 5 was the cause of it.

Gorilla Cagle was one of the most ardent. Beside his self-imposed task as guardian of Diane, he promptly became Operator 5's loyal champion the moment he heard the first whispers against his chief.

"It seems to me that even fellows as little as you ought to have better sense than to believe such rot," he flung contemptuously at a throng of Jimmy's traducers. "Where would this country be if it wasn't for Operator 5? Who would have pulled you out from under the heel of Emperor Rudolph and the Purple Empire. Who would have saved your necks only a month ago when this Kasuga-Tosa gent was ready to burn hell out of the lot of you? Operator 5 could have been President years ago if he'd wanted to—you know that. And now you peanut-brains think he's playing politics to put a stuffed shirt like Tobey into office. Get some size, mugs, and then maybe your brains will grow so that you'll be able to do some *thinking!*"

His impromptu lectures were not always as politely worded as that, and he was more than ready to pitch in whenever he found a group that had come to blows. All morning he ranged up and down the line, grim-faced and ready to snap the head off anyone who dared to insinuate that Operator 5 was not the salt of the earth—but by early afternoon his enemies caught up with him. Any three or four, or even half dozen, of them he could have handled with ease. But twenty were too many; especially when they were armed with clubs and even used pistol barrels to good effect.

They waylaid him behind one of the cook-tents, but the Gorilla soon brought the battle out into the open. Nine of them lay sprawled on the ground with battered faces and broken jaws before he went down—and even then he was by no means out.

Up onto his feet he bounced again, to dispose of three more before they bore him down by sheer weight.

Groggy and only half-conscious, he was staggering back onto his knees when Diane arrived with a detail of military police.

"Seven feet of man—and I let these peanut-brains rough-house me!" he muttered an apology through cracked and bleeding lips before he lost consciousness and was taken to the hospital....

IT WAS while he was there, barely conscious, that the Japanese launched their drive. Convinced that their positions were secure and that the Orientals were checkmated, the Americans had not been as watchful as the moment demanded. Operator 5 and the situation in Washington right then, was the subject uppermost in people's minds.

And then the Japanese struck.... Not with the air-armada that could no longer penetrate the American aerial defense. Without warning the Orientals came over the top of their entrenchments; without a barrage or even the usual clouds of all-enveloping smoke that shrouded their movements. It was nothing more than a hazy mist that hovered over their lines— but death struck witheringly from them.

Soundless death and appalling destruction! Men died in winrows, whole sections of concrete entrenchments crumbled to ruin, steel plates disintegrated—and what a few minutes before had been a supposedly impregnable line suddenly became a ruin, a shambles, over which the blank-faced hordes of know-nothing men came charging!

"Ray-projectors!" General Thayer gasped, as he stood outside his headquarters and viewed the havoc through field-glasses. "That is the only answer. They have some sort of projectors that are more deadly than anything they have been using. Nothing seems to be able to stand before them!"

In a wild rout the survivors of that front line turned and ran for their lives. The second line gave way almost as quickly—and the panic spread to the reserves even before they were called to the front. Not only at one point—apparently the *entire* line had crumbled. Wherever General Thayer turned his glasses, nothing but chaos met his gaze—a rout even worse than those that had preceded the construction of this defense line.

"It's all gone—our work of weeks swept away in less than five minutes!" he groaned as the panic-stricken rabble, that had been an army swirled by his headquarters. "Nothing can save us now!"

But there was at least one on that field of disaster who did not agree with him. Diane Elliot stared at the calamitous rout, with horrified eyes. Well she realized what it meant; realized the unprotected cities that would be wide open to the invader once this steel and concrete bastion was destroyed. It could not be destroyed! This wild stampede must be stopped; the entrenchments must be retaken, *held*—somehow!

If nobody else would do it, she would!

"The enemy is *this* way!" she shouted. She ran into the midst of that wild-eyed throng and pointed toward the on-coming Japanese and know-nothing men. "Operator 5 isn't here to lead you, but I am taking his place! Operator 5's men—this way!"

For a moment it seemed that she might succeed. Half a dozen, then a dozen, men stopped running and rallied around her. In a few moments they numbered a score—fifty. Now they were headed the other way—toward the oncoming enemy.

"Operator 5's men, this way!" her challenge rang out above the tumult—and nearly three hundred grim-faced, desperate-eyed men were following her when the ranks of the know-nothing men engulfed them.

Three hundred against untold thousands! They made a dent in that oncoming wave, carved a way through it, regained a few hundred square yards of ground—then they were lost in the irresistible tide that swept over them. For a moment it had seemed that Diane's desperate charge might swing the tide, but now the demoralized army failed her.

Her heroic handful were overwhelmed, carried to the ground by sheer weight—and then pounced upon by so many of the know-nothing men that they could scarcely move a muscle. Through the second and third ranks of that blank-faced horde, Diane fought her way. Then her automatic was empty, her gun-wrist gripped by a brawny hand.

Frantically she tried to tear loose, but her feet were swept out from under her. They had hold of her legs, her arms—a dozen of them, it seemed; holding her helpless and taking her to the rear, where Moto Taronago and Hachibu Aiko would be waiting....

NEARLY TEN miles that shattered line was pushed back before General Thayer and his officers were able to reorganize it, and then it was only the coming of nightfall that put an end to the American rout. Once the momentum of the retreat was stopped the panic subsided, then the back-breaking work of digging in began. All night long they labored with picks and shovels, throwing up entrenchments, filling sandbags, erecting any sort of a barricade to protect them from the weapons that had already destroyed the finest entrenchments their engineers had been able to construct!

"It is futile," Hugh Thayer despairingly admitted to his staff, "but at least it keeps their minds occupied. Unless we keep them busy they will have time to think—and then there will be no stopping the route from here to the Atlantic coast!"

That was the situation the next morning. Fearfully the fear-stricken troops watched the new day dawn, watched the sun come up brightly. Eight o'clock… eight-thirty… nine; at any moment now that gray mist would arise over the Japanese lines—and then death and destruction would come pouring from them.

The officers could see that shuddering thought in every face; could see their men desperately clinging to their courage and trying hard not to fail. It was not that these men were afraid of death. It was once more the same terrifying specter they had fought against for weeks—the prospect of having to face weapons against which there was no defense, of meeting a fate that was more horrifying than any threat of the grave.

But the line officers were not the only ones who were having their troubles that morning. Back in the field hospital a private war was going on. Three doctors had examined Gorilla Cagle and ruled that he must stay in bed. But it was taking the combined efforts of half a dozen nurses and as many orderlies to keep him there.

And then they did not succeed.

"Seven feet of man—and they expect me to lie here in bed because I have a few scratches!" he roared his indignation.

"Those 'few scratches' happen to be three broken ribs, a nicked skull, half a dozen bad cuts and a leg that you can hardly stand on," one of the nurses corrected, as she pushed him back onto his pillow.

After that the big fellow seemed to subside. He growled and grunted a lot, but the hospital staff sighed with relief when they saw that he had fallen asleep. The nurses relaxed their vigilance and the orderlies left his cot—and the next thing they knew Gorilla Cagle, fully dressed and sporting a head bandage that made him look like a beturbaned Hindu, was striding out of the building with a broad grin!

To keep him on his cot until his broken ribs mended, the doctors had given him a heavy dose of sleeping drops the day before. Under their influence Gorilla Cagle had slept through the Japanese drive, had been carried farther to the rear with the other hospital patients, and had had no idea of what had happened at the front. When he tried to find his old position in the line and discovered that there was no line he stared in open-mouthed amazement.

Finally he managed to locate his squad-mates and jumped down into the makeshift trench beside them. It was after nine o'clock, and every man was on edge, every eye watching the Japanese lines fearfully. His mates had little disposition to answer his questions at that tense moment, but gradually he began to understand what had happened—and then his attention was caught by a group of officers who were arguing a short distance from where he was standing.

"There is nothing to do but withdraw, Colonel," a severe-faced man with the collar-marks of a major was saying. "I know that we dug in here last night, but the position is not tenable. When the Japanese come over, this trench will be as good as nothing—"

"But if we yield it now we will have nothing," Colonel Pollard was protesting. "In the open we will have absolutely no chance—and we *have* to hold this line. You know that. If we are driven back again Chicago is doomed, and after that all of America."

THAT DISCUSSION had attracted the attention of the men, Cagle saw. Not only he, but dozens of others were listening to every word—with mingled emotions. There were about two hundred and fifty of them in this particular stretch of trench—two hundred and fifty men poised there to make a desperate attempt to hold a precarious line that was the last barrier between the enemy and all the rest of America....

Those significant facts percolated into Gorilla Cagle's brain. If he understood this situation correctly, those two hundred and fifty were as good as dead; the Japanese would come over sooner or later and crush them at will—and yet they were standing there, waiting.

"You can't hope to hold this line, Colonel," the major was repeating insistently. "You have no weapons that will combat these new ray-projectors, no equipment that is a match for that of the Japanese. I need not remind you that it is considered good tactics to withdraw and conserve your strength in the face of preponderantly superior armament."

"You're right, Kent—I am not questioning that," the colonel capitulated regretfully. "I hate to give the order, but we will withdraw."

That was where Gorilla Cagle took a hand in the conference.

"Pardon me, Colonel," he interrupted, "but we're not backing up, are we? We're not giving up the line and letting the slant-eyes through?"

"There doesn't seem to be much else we can do, Cagle," Pollard said wearily. "We haven't the weapons!"

"*We* haven't," Cagle's deep voice boomed throughout the length of the trench, "but *they* have over there, haven't they? And they're going to use them on us unless we get hold of them first, right? Then what are we standing here for?" He turned to his mates. "You're going to be killed if you stay here—the major will tell you that. And you'll be killed if you give up this trench and let the Japs through—not only you, but millions more Americans will be killed.

"Seems to me like we need those ray-projectors, don't we? Then what are we standing here for? Let's go over and get them!" he hurled his challenge. "You fellows who ganged up on me yesterday—how many of you have the guts to follow seven feet of man over there into that nest of slant-eyes? I'm going—how many of you are with me?"

He was climbing up over the edge of the trench, standing there above them, taunting them—a gigantic figure clutching a rifle that looked like a child's toy in his hand.

"Cagle!" Colonel Pollard called sharply, but Gorilla Cagle's roaring blast drowned him out.

"I'm going!" Cagle shouted—and he swung on his heel and started on a low, crouching run now for the Japanese trench!

That wild charge was mad, foolhardy, suicidal. He never had a chance; was doomed from the start. One blast from one of those deadly ray-projectors and he would have been cut down—but the ray-projectors were not turned upon him.

From behind their sandbag-piled entrenchments, the Japanese gazed with incredulous eyes. Fascinated, they stared at that roaring bull of a man, that great giant who came running at them as if he would take the world in his great arms and tear it into little pieces.

But when that fantastic charge had covered half the distance between the two lines, uneasy fear suddenly gripped the Orientals. There was something queer, something uncanny, about this snarling, glaring behemoth. Snatching up their rifles, they started pouring shots into him, like hunters trying to bring down a trumpeting bull-elephant.

Bullets hit Gorilla Cagle from every direction. Lead plowed into his body, drilled through his arms, his legs. He was hit time and again—and yet he kept coming on and took more. He should have been a dead man a dozen times over. It was impossible that he could still be alive—*and yet there he was, coming on!*

"Seven feet of man!" his outlandish battle-cry bellowed out over their heads—and suddenly his amazing exhibition of primeval strength and courage struck terror into the hearts of the Japanese.

That madman could not be human! He came on despite everything—and in a few more steps he would be over the top, would have his great hands upon their throats! The terrified Orientals forgot all about their ray-projectors at that moment; they thought of nothing but getting away before that berserk destroyer reached them.

They started scrambling frantically from their trenches— and suddenly there was a wild yell from the trenches of the Americans. Not only the two hundred and fifty who were in Gorilla's Cagle's sector, but men all along the line had been breathlessly watching that astounding exhibition of utter fearlessness. Impetuously, without waiting for orders, they swarmed over the top. With ringing cheers they charged across No Man's Land to the barricades that, only a few minutes before, had looked to them like the very gates of hell.

Gorilla Cagle went down at last. For a moment he seemed to be finished, but somehow in that huge frame was another source of strength which he tapped. Once more he was on his feet, staggering and stumbling now, but going on… on… steadily on, until he had reached his destination. Not until he stood on the edge of the Japanese trench—a trench now in the hands of the victorious Americans—did he crumple and slump inertly.

His job was done.

For a distance of over a mile that enemy trench, with its destructive weapons lying where the terrified Japanese had left them, was in the hands of the Americans when Colonel Pollard knelt beside the fallen giant. For over a mile those deadly ray-projectors had been swung around and were decimating the ranks of the stampeding Orientals.

That was Gorilla Cagle's hour—his moment under the bright lights of eternal glory; and he rose to the occasion like the trouper that he was.

"Seven feet of man..." he gasped; and then the last breath of life went out of that marvelous, super-human bullet-riddled body.

"You were perfectly right, Kent." Colonel Pollard's voice was husky as he turned to the impeccable major, "Nobody could have done this thing—but Gorilla Cagle did it. He turned what promised to be an utter rout into a glorious victory—and he didn't know anything about the manual of tactics. He only knew that he was an *American!*"

They were still there in the Japanese trench when Operator 5's plane landed from Washington and he came running to the battlefield. Gorilla Cagle was dead, but the feat that he performed that day would live on for generations after him. And as he looked down at that bullet-torn body, Operator 5 recalled that day in the hills behind Los Angeles when on no more than a whim he had decided to take the big fellow along with him— and wondered whether there was not something beyond the ken of mortal men that directs their destinies when the fate of a free nation is at stake....

Heaven sends heroes!

CHAPTER 11
ONE LIFE TO GIVE

THAT UNEXPECTED setback, and the loss of scores of their new super-ray projectors, had halted the Japanese advance. For the rest of that day they had made no attempt to go forward. But when night fell, and the Americans were once more working frantically to consolidate their positions, Operator 5 was not deceived into imagining that the menace was past. He had far too high a respect for the Yellow Vulture and too thorough a knowledge of Japanese tenacity and resourcefulness. This was no more than a breathing spell, he knew; a breathing spell after which they might expect—*what?*

Some new form of frightfulness? Some new weapon.

Into Operator 5's thoughts came a reminder of that day in Hachibu Aiko's headquarters when the general had so confidently predicted that if Chicago resisted the Japanese advance the city would be subdued with weapons such as the world had never seen. The moment he had heard that the defense line had crumbled, and the invaders were pushing on toward the Mid-Western metropolis, that threat had recurred to him. He had started wondering what the nature of those weapons might be.

These new ray-projectors? No, because they had made their appearance before Hachibu Aiko had had a defiant city with which to contend. There was some other devilment hatching behind the enemy lines, something else about which he ought to know about—and Operator 5 wrestled earnestly with himself to be sure that he followed the path of duty.

Diane was somewhere behind the enemy lines, and his every inclination was to rush to her assistance, to make every effort to locate and free her. But conscience whispered that his duty was here with the men, bolstering the line and doing everything in his power to make it the impregnable barrier America so badly needed....

The path of duty seemed to be even more clearly defined the next morning, when a telegraph message arrived from Norman King, in Washington. Jimmy read it—and then reread it with hard, narrowed eyes.

"Hold the line at any cost," King urged. "Our experiments going very well. On the verge of a discovery that may mean the turning point you have been hoping for."

Hold the line—that meant stay right here and dig in with the men, Jimmy told himself doggedly. Doc King was on the verge of a discovery that would free those thousands of poor, vacant-eyed devils who were brainless pawns in the hands of the Japanese—a discovery that would break Hachibu Aiko's power and put an end to the menace of the invaders. Operator 5 had no right to endanger that by leaving now.

What would have happened to Diane by that time? Jimmy resolutely closed his mind to that torturing thought and started out for a tour of inspection of the rapidly rebuilding line. Feverish activity greeted him wherever he went, men toiling and sweating at the entrenchments while keen-eyed lookouts kept their glasses trained on the distant Japanese line. Activity everywhere, but no sign of hostilities until he had more than half completed his rounds—when a lookout suddenly hailed him.

"Operator 5, there's something going on out there!" he called excitedly. "A man—he just climbed out of the Jap trench! Here he comes—making for our line!"

Jimmy was up beside the lookout immediately, his own glasses clapped to his eyes. Now he could see the fugitive clearly; could see him darting from side to side, jackrabbiting frantically, as a hail of shots broke loose from behind him and pocked the ground all around him. He could never make it to the American line through that leaden shower; not a chance. Any moment he must go down... and then he *did*.

The lookout sighed as that skipping, darting figure pitched to the ground and lay still. But in a moment the man was on his feet again; was making a desperate spurt; and now Operator 5 caught a glimpse of his face. Ken Williams—one of his own men!

It seemed a miracle that the man was still alive, but he seemed to bear a charmed life—until he was within fifty feet of the American entrenchments. Then suddenly he rose up on tiptoes in his agony, and half a dozen bullets tore through him, slapped him down onto the ground.

After that there was silence from the opposing trench. Not a shot was fired—but Operator 5 knew that trap too well.

"Stay where you are!" he called a sharp warning up and down the trench. "They're only waiting for you to try to get him. There isn't a chance in the world of reaching him."

THEN HE turned to Williams. The man was still alive but so badly wounded that he could not even crawl. He could barely lift his head—until Jimmy called his name. Then his clenched fingers fastened in turf and he managed to turn so that his voice would carry to the line he had not been able to reach.

"Operator 5!" he gasped. "Almost got through—but they uncovered me. Diane Elliot—Aiko has her. They condemned her last night. Going to kill her—blow her to pieces—with a new twen...!"

That was where the waiting Japanese lost their patience. Convinced that the Americans were not going to nibble at the bait stretched so invitingly in front of their trench, the Oriental sharpshooters went into action—and a volley of bullets whistled out over No Man's Land; bullets that thudded into Ken Williams' body and smashed through his skull.

"Better than having to lie out there a couple of hours," the lookout at Jimmy's elbow muttered pityingly; but as Operator 5 turned away he could not help wishing that Ken Williams' agony had lasted for a few seconds longer, until he had finished that all-important message.

Diane had been condemned to death! That torturing knowledge screamed at him. Diane had been condemned to death! The Japanese were going to blow her to pieces with a "new twent...." The last two syllables that had fallen from Ken Williams' lips went through Jimmy's mind again and again. Frantically he tried to finish the sentence that was now locked forever behind the undercover man's dead lips.

Some fiendish sort of execution device, undoubtedly. But suddenly it occurred to him that this might be one of the new weapons Hachibu Aiko had promised to loose against Chicago!

Whatever that weapon was, he wanted to know about it before it was tried out—before Diane Elliot gave it its baptism of blood!

There was nothing more that he could do there on the defense line that General Thayer could not attend to, he told himself swiftly—but now he knew that there *was* something he could do beyond the Japanese lines! Something that he *must* do!

He must make his way into that territory immediately, without waiting another hour. But how? The lines were now so closely watched from both sides that it was hopeless to try to negotiate No Man's Land before nightfall—and that was still nearly a full day away. A day during which anything might happen to Diane!

To attempt to penetrate enemy territory by air was equally hopeless; his plane would be brought down before it had crossed the trenches. Yet surely, along all those miles of battlefront, there must somewhere be a loophole through which he could slip. Somewhere the Japanese....

And then he had it!

During that mad charge yesterday morning, some Japanese prisoners had been taken, among them one of the fed officers the Americans had captured. Ito Nadeyoshi.... Operator 5 had questioned him the night before; learned the man's regiment and something of his personal history; noticed, also, that the Oriental's features were not radically different from his own.

Ito Nadeyoshi! His uniform would fit Jimmy, and his features would be fairly easy to duplicate with makeup. Now the plan was beginning to form itself. Ten miles or so to the south, there was a point where a small thicket lay between the lines—an ideal exit for an escaping prisoner!

Promptly Jimmy went to work. Within half an hour he was clad in Nadeyoshi's uniform and had so transformed his appearance that he needed a bodyguard as he started down the defense line to the jumping-off place. There he gathered his squad of volunteers around him and carefully explained their roles—as fraught with danger as his own.

An outbreak of shots was the overture. In the midst of the fusillade Jimmy climbed out of the trench and started on a crazy, zigzag course for the thicket. After him came a dozen Americans, their bullets plowing up the ground all around him. Desperately he whirled and fired at them, dropped them to the ground and gained sufficient time to reach the cover of the trees. Then they were after him, and the thicket reverberated with the sound of shots and pounding feet. The Japanese had seen it—had fallen for the bait!

Out of their trench leaped a score of the little yellow men, and in another moment they had reached the small stand of trees. After that, there was no pretense. The Americans shot to kill. Hand to hand they battled furiously, desperately holding the attention of the rescue party and giving Operator 5 time to reach the enemy lines.

With a dozen of the "rescuing" infantrymen around him, Jimmy covered the last few yards and flung himself over the trench parapet—to meet the real test. A young officer was there to meet him almost as soon as he arrived; a wide-eyed lieutenant who had a dozen questions to ask and was all ears for details of his capture and escape.

"There is little time now for conversation," Jimmy told him politely. "I have seen things which must be brought to the ears of the Honorable Habuchi Aiko. I must get back to headquarters without delay."

"Certainly," his welcomer agreed instantly. "I should have thought of that. There is a car here, a short distance behind the line, that will speed your journey. I shall appoint you a driver and an escort."

A driver.... An escort.... Jimmy looked searchingly into the yellow face, but the almond eyes appeared to be guileless. The lieutenant was not suspicious; he was merely being infernally helpful. There was nothing for it but to accept his arrangements. WITH A Japanese infantryman at the wheel and two more in the seat behind him, "Ito Nadeyoshi" set out for General Aiko's headquarters, in the style to which his rank entitled him—while his fast-working brain desperately sought a way to rid himself of the Orientals. There seemed to be none that would not arouse immediate suspicion.

Swiftly the miles sped past, and he could figure no escape short of attempting to get the drop on the three of them—which was almost impossible from where he was sitting. Dangerous, too, because now they were constantly passing other Japanese on the road.

No, he decided grimly, there was nothing to do but go through with it; nothing but to be escorted into Habuchi Aiko's presence and stand the searching scrutiny of Moto Taronago's keen eyes.

But just as they reached the village that was now the Japanese headquarters there was a respite. Out from one of the buildings marched a squad of soldiers with a lieutenant at their head, and between their ranks walked an American with his arms tied behind his back. A spy!

"Wait here," Jimmy ordered the driver. "I would see the death of this fellow." And before they could answer he had the door open and was striding to join the small crowd that was gathering around the execution place.

Who was that poor devil? Another of his own men? Operator 5's heart went out to the condemned man as he followed the death-marching squad—and then he stared in amazement. There was no mistaking that face. Any young woman in America would have recognized it immediately. Ralph Baylor, the motion picture star!

His handsome face white and set in lines more grim than he ever had assumed for the silver screen, Baylor walked to his place against a brick wall and turned to face the Japanese rifles. This was an execution of more than ordinary importance, Jimmy noted; besides the usual squad commander two other officers had accompanied the firing-squad.

"You have one more opportunity to reconsider your decision," one of these now addressed him. "You were apprehended while on your way through our territory from the Pacific states. You were bringing a message from General Butler to Operator 5. All that we require is that you reveal the contents of that message; then your life will be spared."

A message from Butler! Now Jimmy understood why he had

not been able to communicate with the western defense head-quarters for the past three days. The Japanese had cut all wire communication and had scrambled the ether so badly that radio was useless. For some reason they did not want him to know what was going on in the west—and Butler had sent Baylor in a desperate attempt to get in and out of the Japanese-held territory.

A few words would have saved Ralph Baylor's life at that moment. The sun was shining brightly, the air was redolent with the fragrance of mid-summer—the sort of a day on which life was well worth living; especially for one with the natural endowments that were Baylor's. But the actor's lips remained firmly pressed together and his eyes never flinched.

"Very well then," the officer drew back with a shrug, and the firing-squad stepped into position, their commander's sharp orders rapped out into the still air.

Helpless to interfere, Operator 5 stood there rooted to the ground, and as his eyes fixed on that set face its features seemed to blur and take on those of a schoolmaster who, two centuries before, had faced a firing-squad with equal calmness and regretted only that he had but one life to sacrifice for his beloved country....

The rifles roared—and like Nathan Hale before him, Ralph Baylor dropped to the ground, his body pierced by eight bullets. For a fraction of a second Jimmy Christopher stopped to gaze down at the crumpled form, and a hard lump welled up into his throat. Never in its most effective poses had that face, which so many American women adored, looked more noble than now when it was bullet-torn and blood-smeared!

RALPH BAYLOR died to preserve the secrets that had been entrusted to him, but his death served his country even more effectively than he knew—for Operator 5 quickly took advantage of that distraction to mingle with the crowd and make his way to the farther side of what he judged to be the headquarters building. There he halted and surveyed the scene swiftly. His chauffeur and escort would be looking for him in a few moments; before then he had to get away from here or find a safe hiding place.

Just beyond him he caught the sound of voices. Several Japanese soldiers were talking. From their conversation he gathered that they were waiting for the arrival of an officer who was to go with them—an officer who was to be freshly assigned to them; one whom they did not know!

Cautiously Jimmy peered around the edge of the building that separated him from them—and stared at a large motor lorry that was loaded with shells of immense size! Shells for a huge naval gun, they appeared to be! And instantly his daring plan was formed!

Circling the headquarters building, he strode arrogantly from the front of it and marched up to the truck. The soldiers sprang to salute and he stepped up into the seat beside the driver, gave the command to proceed—and the lorry started down the road, headed for—*where?*

Headed for the gun that would shoot those huge shells, and away from the piercing eyes of the Yellow Hawk—that was all that Operator 5 needed to know. In a few moments the head-quarters settlement was behind them and the lorry was rumbling in a southeasterly direction into northern Illinois.

As the miles sped past, his interest and his excitement increased. The lorry was heading straight in the direction of Chicago!

Finally it drew up beneath a heavily camouflaged, tent-like netting that covered nearly an acre of ground just beyond the deserted town of Millbrook. Beneath that tremendous awning were thousands of those huge shells—sufficient to sink the navies of the world; sufficient to wipe the entire city of Chicago off the map!

But Millbrook was at least fifty miles from the metropolis; no gun could throw shells that far. These must be for some other diabolical purpose. What that might be, Jimmy intended to discover promptly.

The moment the lorry drew up beside the netting-covered area his men began to unload their cargo, and he started out ostensibly for the old-fashioned mansion that was being used as a headquarters building. Instead, he skirted the house and went on past it, toward a stretch of woods where he could see quite a number of men moving around. That clump of woods, he found, was close to the edge of a steep bluff, more than two hundred feet high, that formed one bank of the Fox River. The American defense line, at this point, was on the other side of the river, the Americans holding the lower bank and the country beyond, while the Japanese held the high bluff that overlooked it.

An almost impregnable position, Jimmy realized, as he looked down over the sheer, rocky, palisade-like cliff to the water below. It would take a human fly to scale that embankment.

The Japanese fully realized the security of their position and had not even bothered to take possession of the narrow fringe of shore on their side of the river. Sufficient for them to hold the unscalable height—and to convert it into a gun emplacement such as the world had never seen!

Operator 5's eyes popped wide with amazement when he went through that wooded clump and stepped out onto the camouflage-protected stretch beyond it. There, like a row of cannon muzzles bristling from the side of an old-time frigate, was a line of tremendous-size guns! Huge naval pieces that were larger than anything he had ever seen. Larger than any sixteen or eighteen-inch gun... and suddenly he knew what Ken Williams had tried to say before he died! "New twen...." Now those incomprehensible syllables made sense. New twenty-inch guns!

Williams had tried to tell him that Diane was to be blown to pieces with one of these new twenty-inch guns!

This was the hellish weapon Hachibu Aiko had been holding up his sleeve to let loose on Chicago. These tremendous guns would easily send their shells a distance of fifty miles. It was to get within range for them that the Japanese drive had been launched—and because Hachibu Aiko was now satisfied with his position that the Orientals were making no further efforts to drive onward!

Operator 5 could picture how Aiko and the Yellow Vulture must be chuckling. Let the stupid Americans hold onto their precious trenches; over their heads these great guns would hurl tons of destruction that would blow to fragments the cities at their backs, would devastate the entire country in their rear!

The Yellow Vulture... the man's evil cunning was diabolical. Every move that he made seemed to have a hidden and little suspected significance. Every time that he met apparent defeat, it was only to come up with a carefully calculated plan that had gone forward uninterrupted....

AS IF the very thought of the wily Oriental was sufficient to conjure him up, Moto Taronago suddenly appeared as if from nowhere. Lovingly he looked at the mammoth guns, with their long, shiny barrels and their heavy metal screens to protect the gunners. Then his beady eyes turned to Jimmy and his vulturine face twisted into a pleased grimace.

"You admire our little one, do you, Captain?" he murmured. "But you will admire them far more when they start to speak tomorrow morning. I think, however, they may not regard them quite so highly in the city of Chicago when our explosive shells begin dropping on their heads and tearing their wonderful town into shattered fragments. It is too bad we cannot be there also, to see those shells land—but I have watched them on the proving ground. The world has never seen such destruction as they will wreak; no, the world has never seen one of its largest cities literally wiped off the map, blown right out of the earth by its very foundations!"

Chuckling in anticipation of the death of millions of helpless people, the Yellow Vulture went from gun to gun, inspecting them carefully, talking with their crews—while chill horror

172

clamped down on Jimmy Christopher. Starkly he visualized that unsuspecting city going about its daily business, when suddenly tons of exploding hell would rain down upon it! There were twenty-five of those tremendous guns—sufficient to pocket the city and turn it into a ghastly death-trap from which there would be no escape for the cowering, fear-maddened victims!

And tied to the mouth of one of those deadly monsters would be the soft body of Diane Elliot....

Somehow, that fiendish program must be thwarted! How he would accomplish that, Jimmy had no idea—*but accomplish it he must!*

It would take days to flank that almost inaccessible position; would mean breaching the Japanese lines above or below the bluff and battling a way to its rear. Days of fighting—if it could be done at all; and those terrible guns would start their deadly thunder in the morning! Days of desperate struggling—when a few hours were all that remained!

There *must* be some other way... and there was. Jimmy looked down over that sheer cliff and could feel the bottom of his stomach flinching. Men *could* climb that almost perpendicular face— and they would have to do it. It was the only alternative....

But first he had to get back to the American lines—and the only way was down that cliff. To attempt to cross farther down, where the trenches were separated only by a waste of No Man's Land, would mean to be shot as a Japanese by his own men. The cliff was the only way—and that would have to wait until dark.

The daylight hours never had seemed to drag as slowly as they did that afternoon. Jimmy did his best to make himself incon-

Slowly the advance of the know-nothing men came on—up to the very guns!

spicuous, fearing that at any moment he would find himself in a position where his disguise must be penetrated. A dozen times he was certain that keen eyes were watching him suspiciously,

but nobody attempted to interfere with him—and at last that long day faded into dusk.

As soon as the shadows were deep enough to afford him concealment, he stole to the edge of the cliff and sat down in a clump of shrubbery. Warily he worked his way farther, until his feet were over the brink—and then he was on his way down. Foot by foot, clinging by his fingertips, grasping bushes that came away in his hands, clutching at rocky edges just in time to keep himself from catapulting headlong.

The way down seemed endless. Dusk deepened into darkness, and then he had to depend entirely upon his sense of touch. Innumerable times he slipped and clung by one hand while he dangled out over nothingness; more than once the earth gave way beneath him and a miniature avalanche threatened to sweep him to destruction. But at last he reached the bottom and was able to wipe the cold perspiration that had been bathing his face.

He had made it—and now remained the worse task of scaling that sheer height from below….

TEN MINUTES later a dripping figure waded out of the Fox River on the American-held bank and was promptly surrounded by a ring of threatening rifles. The men behind those rifles didn't like Japanese, and they needed only an excuse for constricting their fingers on the triggers—but the swimmer gave them no opportunity.

"Don't look much like it, I know, but I am Operator 5," he told them. "Take me back to your commander as fast as we can get there."

Operator 5! That magic name had attracted a crowd before

he reached the section headquarters hut, where Colonel Douglas Hazelton was in command. Before their wondering eyes the dye washed out of Jimmy's hair, the high Japanese cheekbones disappeared, his eyes lost their almond cast, his skin shed its olive hue—and he was the leader they all recognized.

"I have been behind the enemy lines, Colonel—and I want to go back there," Jimmy spoke quickly. "Tonight, as soon as we can get started. I want volunteers to go with me. Five hundred. Men who can climb. We are going up the face of the cliff opposite your line."

"But that's impossible!" Hazelton protested. "A mountain goat couldn't get up or down that cliff!"

"I don't know about a mountain goat, Colonel," Jimmy grinned, "but I just came down it—and I'm going back up. We *have* to go back up." He turned to the men. "On top of that cliff are twenty-inch guns that will open fire on Chicago tomorrow morning. Guns that can throw terrific explosive shells fifty miles. Do you realize what that means? Can you picture what is going to happen in Chicago—unless we stop it? Can you picture those close-packed streets, those square blocks filled with women and kids—when those shells start bursting among them?"

They could picture that appalling scene. He saw it in their narrowed eyes, their tense faces—and he struck while the iron was hot.

"We can put an end to that scheme tonight—by doing what the Japanese consider the impossible," he appealed to them. "We can scale that cliff—and once we are on top of it we can rout the Japs before they know what is happening. It is our chance to save not only Chicago but all America from destruction. I am going back up there. How many of you are going with me?"

There was not a dissenting voice in that whole assemblage—except Colonel Hazelton's.

"I don't think we need volunteers for this, Operator 5," he said quietly; "the regiment will go with you. But there is one suggestion I want to make—and take this from an experienced mountain-climber. Wait until dawn. We can cross the river in the dark, but very few of us will reach the top of that cliff without the aid of at least a little light. If we start as soon as the darkness breaks we can be at the crest before the Japs are out of their blankets."

Jimmy chafed at the bit during those long hours of the night, but he put them to good advantage by talking with the men, supervising their equipment, planning the strategy for the morrow and building up in them a morale that would have sent them after him into the gates of hell itself.

In the darkness they forded the Fox quietly, and then huddled on the meager left bank until the blackness had turned gray and the eastern sky was beginning to crimson. Not until then—until the rocky formation of the cliff was clearly discernible—did he give the word. Then that great climb began. Over a stretch of more than five hundred yards they started to work their way upward, slowly, cautiously, foot by foot—men who knew that a misstep meant certain death.

"Stony Point had nothing on this cliff, Operator 5!" Colonel Hazelton panted, as he tried to keep pace with his leader. "They ought to call you 'Mad Jimmy' after this!"

Mad Jimmy! And the nickname would have been a worthy

companion for that other "mad" hero who stormed the sheer, rugged height of the Hudson River's Stony Point. Mad Anthony Wayne was another American who would not admit that a thing could not be done, when it had to be done....

Steadily they climbed, foot by foot, yard by yard—until at last the impossible was accomplished, and the first of them crawled over the edge. Four or five... a dozen... scores... and then hundreds reached their objective, until nearly the entire thousand men who had followed him were at Operator 5's back.

It was not until then that the amazed Japanese realized what had happened while they slept; not until a sentry fired his rifle to sound the alarm—and tumbled them out of their blankets to meet a blistering hail of American lead. The half-awakened Japanese fell back, routed, before that onslaught—and Operator 5 pushed his advantage for all it was worth.

There would not be much time; he knew that, and he had counted heavily on the element of surprise to sweep them through the Japanese camp and out to the big gun emplacements. His plan was working! The Orientals were running, were putting up hardly any resistance! They would be routed from the guns and pushed over the cliff!

But at that moment a whistle cut through the dawn, loud and clear—a whistle that knifed into Jimmy and chilled his blood. The Yellow Vulture! Things had been going entirely too smoothly; he ought to have expected some kind of trick!

THAT SHRILL blast had two immediate effects—and instantly Jimmy saw that his fears were fully realized. Out from beneath the big guns swarmed a host of guards, who must have been posted there day and night; guards who greeted the on-coming Americans with a hail of machine-gun fire and a bombardment of hand grenades. The sudden appearance of those guards was sufficient to check the charge—and then, from the direction of the field of net-covered shells, came the men who would repulse it; who would hurl the Americans back over the cliff whence they had come!

The Yellow Vulture was taking no chances with his precious guns. As usual, he had thought of everything and had made his diabolically thorough preparations to meet any emergency.

The Americans were driven back by that onslaught. The machine-guns on one side, the charging Japanese reserves on another, and the routed sleepers hurriedly reorganizing and swinging into action—it was too much. Outnumbered more than three to one, Jimmy's men gave ground slowly, stubbornly—but they retreated, nevertheless.

The *coup* had failed! Instead of saving Chicago, Jimmy had merely thrown away a thousand lives!

But at that moment Moto Taronago pushed his advantage too far. Out from wherever they had been holding her captive, his men dragged Diane Elliot. Dragged her into the midst of the fray, to the mouth of one of the big guns—and thrust her, feet first, into it!

Slowly that terrible long muzzle turned, until it was aimed right at the fleeing Americans. Behind the metal shield at its rear the Japanese swarmed, their grinning faces looking out as a small motorized truck came trundling up with one of the huge shells. Half a dozen of them grabbed the great cylinder, were barely able to lift it—and shoved it home in the firing chamber. The breech snapped closed.

That much Operator 5 saw—and then he went berserk. Charging, head down, through the ranks of his own men, he hurled himself at the Orientals. Bullets spat all around him, tore through his clothing, burned his neck and his arms—but he went on; and after him came the men who, a moment before, had been on the verge of panic. Diane Elliot's terrified face projecting from that gun muzzle had been just the tonic they needed to restore their control and to fill their hearts with fierce, white-hot rage!

Now the grenades meant nothing to them; the machine-guns no longer daunted them. Straight at the guns they charged, sweeping the machine-gunners out of the way, turning their own weapons against them. Straight up to the guns—to swarm over the crew who were trying to fire the one in which Diane lay helpless.

That gun crew went down to a man, and so did another that sprang up to take the fallen men's places. There was a ring of dead Americans around the weapons breech—but the gun was not fired until Operator 5 had managed to drag Diane from the barrel and had cut her free.

A mighty cheer rose from those American throats the moment she sprang clear and grabbed up a rifle one of the men had dropped. Irresistibly they surged forward, sweeping the Japanese before them. Now the machine-guns were all in American hands, were blasting a withering fire into the ranks of the fleeing Orientals.

After them the Americans went—but not all of them. That, Operator 5 had carefully arranged beforehand. While the main body of his men kept the Japanese at bay, the others set to work with the contents of deadly packages they had carried up that sheer cliff on their backs. Dynamite and nitro-glycerine!

Swiftly they set their charges around those big guns, set them in the floor of the cliff itself—and then joined their mates in a charge that drove the disorganized Japanese back into their disordered camp. With a thunderous detonation, the first of those charges went off—to be echoed by another and another. Dozens of them that shook the atmosphere as if the big guns themselves were speaking.

But when that heroic blasting was finished, there were no more big guns on the cliff; a good part of the cliff itself was no more. In a wildly tumbling avalanche, guns and crumbled rock were crashing down into the bed of the Fox far below. Where there had been a sheer cliff, there was now a steep hill that gave way beneath their feet and set them rolling and tumbling when they started down—but to those victorious Americans the descent was a lark, almost an amusement-park holiday.

In a solid, death-dealing line the machine-gunners and dynamiters held the crest until the rest had gone. Then, with a parting salvo to slow up the Japanese advance, they too piled over the edge in a mad slide that skidded them all the way down and into the muddy waters of the rock-and-dirt-choked Fox. Back across the now narrow stream the heroic survivors swam—while spiteful bullets spattered harmlessly about them, like the snarling curses that must have been spewing from the lips of the Yellow Vulture!

CHAPTER 12
AMERICANS, HOLD
THAT LINE!

MOTO TARONAGO'S diabolical plan for the utter annihilation of Chicago had been thwarted, but that only increased his relentless determination to take the city and raze it as an object lesson to the rest of America. As soon as the threat of the twenty-inch guns were eliminated, the Japanese attacks on the American lines began again with redoubled vigor. Plainly, the invaders were resolved to take the city by storm—and now it was the American captives, the pathetic know-nothing men and women, who bore the brunt of the furious onslaught.

Using them as shock troops, the Japanese hurled them against the American positions by the thousands—until the frightful carnage sickened the harried defenders. Crouching low in their trenches to avoid the lethal blast of the ray-projectors, they were fairly inundated by waves of the blank-faced people; had to cut them down mercilessly in order to save themselves from being captured and meeting a like fate. "This is the most barbaric outrage the world has ever seen!" General Thayer gritted his indignation. "We have to kill these poor creatures for our own self-preservation—but it's like slaughtering sheep; except that these aren't sheep but our own people!"

183

All America shuddered in horrified revulsion as that ghastly massacre went on, and in millions of minds the same question was uppermost—how soon would the frightful scourge reach them? How soon would it be their turn to become one of those fearsome creatures, a living corpse that must roam the earth doing the bidding of foreign masters until a fellow-countryman was forced to end its ignominy?

Throughout the land that horror stalked like an appalling specter about which nothing could be done. But in Washington the most outstanding scientific and medical experts of the country worked tirelessly trying to find an answer to that baffling condition. Day after day Tim Donovan sat in the laboratory among them and knew no more about what was going on around him than if he were sleeping with his eyes open. Test after test they tried upon him, experiment after experiment—and always the heartbreaking answer was the same: *failure!*

Day after day—until one night when, just as the tired experimenters were about to give up and go to bed, Tim reacted with a faint show of interest, of new understanding! Like hounds on a fresh scent, those weary men gathered around him; and they were still there in the morning when the sun was high in the sky—but now their eyes were sparkling and their faces were flushed with excitement.

"I think we've done it, gentlemen," Norman King said gravely, as he cradled Tim Donovan's sleeping form in the crook of his arm. "We have brought Tim back out of the shadow—and if we could do it for him, we can do it for those countless thousands now under the Japanese yoke!" Five minutes later he was at the telephone, waiting for his call to go through to Operator 5; waiting to voice the message that would put new spirit and determination in the wavering American resistance.

"We have what you want, Operator 5!" the good news throbbed into Jimmy Christopher's ear. "We have cured Tim and are developing an instrument that will take care of the rest of the afflicted victims. All that we need is time—time to round out this invention and to put it into production. If you can only hold your lines a little while longer—a week at the most—I will give you a weapon that will defeat the Japanese!"

Hold the line! That became the American watchword along a battleline nearly eight hundred miles in length. Hold the line! Men who had been ready to give up and flee anywhere, just so that they were going away from that dread menace, rallied to the battle-cry and resisted every foot of the Japanese advance fiercely.

Desperately the exhausted defenders dug in more deeply and threw back assault after assault. Slowly, yard by yard, mile by mile, they yielded; but now the Japanese achieved no rout. This was no panic-stricken foe they drove before them. These were men who knew that they would be victorious if only they could hold out long enough.

Men and women, too; for now there were hundreds of wives and mothers helping to replace the depleted reserves. Under the leadership of Mary Reid, they had taken over many duties behind the line in order to release hundreds of men for the trenches.

The national army had long since been reorganized and

augmented by thousands of volunteers. Those regiments had been stretched out from the Great Lakes to Memphis. The militia regiments had been blended with them and had lost their identity in the common cause. Equally mingled were the divisions of Canadians that Sir John Bacon had sent marching in through Detroit. Hundreds of thousands of men—but the toll of the Japanese and their mindless shock troops was appalling. Hachibu Aiko had set himself to wage a war of attrition, and mercilessly he pursued it—a war that would not cease until America was bled so white of her manhood that surrender would no longer be necessary.

That day must never come, Operator 5 resolved grimly—but as he scanned the mounting losses he wondered how much longer they could hold out. The men were keeping the line intact, but it was being pushed back steadily no matter how bravely they fought.... Particularly in the sector west of Chicago. That was taking the brunt of the assault—and was gobbling up troops in dismaying numbers.

A week, Norman King had asked for, and on the night of the sixth day Operator 5 knew that it was nothing short of a miracle that they were still grimly holding on.

CANNY HACHIBU AIKO was well aware of conditions behind the American lines, and he, too, must have sensed that one more day would seal the fate of Chicago and the United States of America. Shortly after dawn the next morning he launched his attack with a savagery that tore holes in the American front in a dozen places. Those gaps were quickly refilled, but by then there were others and others. Gap after gap, until it seemed that the whole line must crumble.

Desperately Jimmy threw in every reserve at his command, stripped the back areas and sent every man there to the front, even weakened the line at points farther north and south in order to bolster up this sagging spot.

The respite this time was less than an hour, and then the Japanese were hammering again; were driving in with wave after wave of the know-nothing people. Charge after charge, that desperate line stood—a line that now seemed to be composed of almost as many women as men.

The telephone the busy Signal Corps men had strung to the gas station shack he was using as his headquarters demanded Operator 5's attention. He grabbed it up subconsciously and jerked it to his ear—and then his eyes widened, his face blanched. His hands were trembling as he sprang up from the table that served him as a desk—and without a word he raced outside and to an army car that stood nearby....

THE OFFICE was empty when frantic General Thayer came in to report that the line had broken wide open at three different points and was falling back. Operator 5 was not there—but Thayer shrugged his shoulders. What matter? What could Operator 5 do now? What could anyone do? This was the end. The line was crumbling. It would hold for perhaps ten minutes more—and then it would give way like a house of cards. Instead of trained troops, those seasoned fighters would become panic-stricken.

But before he witnessed that miserable end he would go out

there and join those who could never again be defeated, Thayer resolved, and he led the surviving members of his staff out into the sagging, hard-pressed line; out to where Mary Reid stood firing a gun that was flanked on both sides by heaps of dead men.

There were women all along that line now—live women and dead ones, too. Sweating over the big seventy-fives, crouching over machine-guns, lying flat behind bulwarks of corpses and using their rifles with deadly effect—Mary Reid's women were carrying on as grimly and stoically as the slaughtered men whose places they filled.

Four times the waves of the know-nothing men had come charging up to those guns and been blown back, only to reform immediately and come on again; four times without a rest. They were not human; were nothing but machines that came on and on as long as they could stand.

Now that dense wave had reformed, was returning again—but this time Mary Reid stood with wide-staring eyes, her jaw dropped open; the face of a woman who has seen a ghost. And she had done just that; she had seen two of them—was staring at them as they came marching straight toward her. Ghosts with lackluster eyes that did not recognize her!

"Emmet! Owen!" the beloved names were a mere whisper as they fell from her white, trembling lips. "Oh, my God!"

They were marching straight toward her, straight into the muzzle of her gun—but after that single moaning supplication to providence, Mary Reid's face hardened and her eyes became as blank and unseeing as theirs. They were helpless, but so was she—and if she failed now thousands of other innocent people might be turned into poor, doomed creatures like them because of her weakness. She could not fail!

Resolutely she gripped the lanyard—but before she could pull it back there was a commotion behind her. Men were running up, were shouting excitedly, and then she recognized the voice of Operator 5.

"Hold it, Mary!" he called to her. "This will be better than your gun!" And he drew her back, away from the loaded fieldpiece.

Astonished, Mary Reid turned to him—and saw that the American lines had opened in half a dozen places; in others at intervals as far as she could see. In those openings men were crouching over some strange new weapons that looked like motion-picture cameras attached to foot-long black cylinders that were several inches in diameter; queer-looking contraptions mounted on sturdy metal tripods.

The muzzles of the cylinders were leveled like guns, and she heard a peculiar whining hum come from the weapons when the operators pressed a trigger-like arrangement and pivoted them from side to side. What she expected to see come from those wide round snouts she did not know—but *nothing* came from them; *nothing at all!*

And yet there must be something—for the know-nothing men were reeling as if they had been hit, were grasping their heads. Their faces were suddenly contorted with pain, and then—they began to look *human!*

"A new ray generator of Norman King's, General," she heard Operator 5 explaining to General Thayer. "They are very powerful shock producers. Played upon the drug-doped brains of those poor devils, *they actually stun them back to normal!"*

But Mary Reid hardly heard that. Emmet was out there— her Emmet, the way he had always been! He was standing there half-dazed, trying to realize where he was and why—and then he saw her, and *he smiled!* He was running toward her, but Mary Reid met him more than half-way. She was sobbing in his arms as Operator 5's voice stabbed into her consciousness.

"The other way, men!" he was shouting. "Behind you are the Japanese who killed your families and made slaves of you! Use your weapons on them! This way—for America!"

"Operator 5!" one of the reclaimed men yelled his recognition, and hundreds of throats took up the cry.

With his automatic waving above his head, Operator 5 charged among them and turned them. Stunned for a moment by that seemingly magical transformation, the men behind the American lines had stood gaping uncertainly—but now they, too, took up the cry. They, too, swarmed forward with the reclaimed men who, a few minutes before, had been their unaccountable foes.

"Operator 5! For America!" the battle-cries rang out all up and down that line, became a chant—a chant of victory as the dumbfounded Japanese broke and fled from a host of grim-faced, vengeful pursuers that now far outnumbered them.

THAT ASSAULT swept the Orientals back so swiftly that they fled for their lives, without any thought of the equipment they were abandoning. Guns, ray-projectors, tanks of the brain-stupefying drug, even many of their huge air monsters fell into the hands of the on-sweeping Americans—but Operator 5 gave those trophies of war hardly a glance. There was just one prize he wanted—and that was the Yellow Vulture!

Straight ahead he led the vanguard of his troops, and so swift was their totally unexpected advance that they swooped down on the old mansion the Japanese were using as a headquarters building before Hachibu Aiko's staff had had time to evacuate. Orientals died by the scores on the steps and the wide front porch as that swirling charge engulfed them—but the firing outside would give Aiko and the Yellow Vulture warning!

Fearful that the leaders would escape, Operator 5 outstripped his men in dashing through the spacious hallway and into a large downstairs room—from which a quick hail of bullets greeted him the moment he entered. Springing back out of the light of the doorway, he hunched forward and the roar of his automatics filled the room with thunder—and with death. Four, five, and then another of those staff officers slumped to the floor in the matter of a few seconds. But that had been sufficient time to allow Hachibu Aiko to dive through a rear door and slam it shut after him.

Aiko and Taronago, too!

Jimmy knew that even before he sprinted out of that room and down a corridor to the rear of the house. The commander was just leaping into an automobile that was already under way; an automobile that streaked off in the direction of several of the huge aircraft—and, as it went, the half-snarling, half-grinning face of the Yellow Vulture peered out through the back window tauntingly!

His two prizes slipped through his fingers, Operator 5 turned dejectedly to the front of the building, and as he passed a moan of agony attracted his attention to the staff room he had just left. That would be one of the men he had shot; small fry of little importance—but, because he could not stand by and see even a barbarous enemy suffer without attention, he stepped into the room.

For an instant he looked around, trying to discover the source of the moan—and then the hair at the back of his neck fairly stood on end! There on his back on the floor lay a man who writhed in his death agony. In a desperate attempt to staunch the wound that was spouting his life blood, he had gotten out of his coat, had torn off most of his shirt to use as a bandage—and then had lost his strength....

The white shirt sleeve lay limp across the lower half of his face, reaching to the bridge of his nose—and as he stared down Jimmy Christopher was looking at the white-masked face of the surgeon who had been the cause of his final trapping in the Los Angeles sanitarium! The face he had seen for a moment in that doorway beside the basement stairs! The face he seemed to remember seeing hanging over him during those long hours when he was only half-conscious!

Jimmy knelt beside him and lifted the torn sleeve from his face, to reveal a countenance that was vaguely familiar.

"You don't recognize me—for who I am, do you, Operator 5?" the elderly man gasped. "But I know you—well. I know every line of your face—so well that I can build others—just like it. Frederick Steckel is my name—Los Angeles specialist—plastic surgeon—one of the best. That is why I had such a fine movie following. Could change them—do anything with them they wanted."

Dr. Frederick Steckel…. Jimmy remembered him now, remembered his name. Steckel had been a member of Mayor Hunter's big-name defense committee, but Jimmy did not remember having seen him in Los Angeles during the hectic days of the plague.

"But once my knife slipped—an illegal operation," Steckel was saying. "That was murder. Enoch Schrader knew about that—held it over my head—made me do whatever he wanted. That was why you were lured to Los Angeles—after Keyes had been killed. So that I could have plenty of time—to use you as a model—to make duplicates of you—for Schrader and Taronago—and Tobey. Schrader had men who greatly resembled you—that made it easy for me. I made them almost your twins."

Steckel was so weak and his breath was so short, his words so difficult, that Jimmy did not like to interrupt; but there were questions, unclear references in the old man's gasping account, that he must have straightened out.

"Schrader and Taronago—and Carman Tobey?" he asked doubtfully. "The three of them worked together?"

"That's what they think—Schrader and Tobey—but they are fools," the surgeon half-whispered. "Taronago—he will be the boss—will control them all for Japan. He will let Schrader—that movie-struck simpleton—be the dressed-up king of a crazy, opéra bouffe kingdom on the Pacific coast. Tobey is to be president—of a puppet republic—in the middle of the country—from Canada to the Gulf."

A kingdom and a second republic carved out of the United States! The man must be mad! But when Jimmy looked into the half-glazed eyes of the dying man, he knew that Frederick Steckel was not crazy. Incredible as it might seem, the old surgeon was in complete possession of his senses....

"But these men you say you made resemble me—there was only one, wasn't there, Steckel?" Jimmy tried to clear up another point that puzzled him. "The one who operated in Los Angeles and then in Washington—"

But no answer came from Frederick Steckel's lips, and when Jimmy bent close he found that he was propping up a corpse. THOUGHTFULLY OPERATOR 5 rose from beside the silent body, and in that moment he knew that the victory he had won that day was indeed a hollow one. The Japanese invasion was stemmed, had been turned into a rout. Chicago was saved—but two-thirds of America was lost! Only the partially ruined East and the South still flew the Stars and Stripes and acknowledged allegiance to the United States of America!

So that was why Moto Taronago could smile tauntingly even in the face of what had seemed to be utter defeat....

With a heavy heart Jimmy Christopher stepped out onto the porch—to be hailed by General Thayer, who had come seeking him. Thayer had with him a man in flying uniform, who proved to be a courier from the South—and not until he had made his report did Jimmy appreciate the full extent of the Yellow Vulture's consummate plotting!

"I have just come from Vicksburg," the flyer repeated what he had already told General Thayer. "All our wires are cut, and there has been no way of notifying you that Texas and Louisiana have been invaded and conquered by an overwhelming force of South Americans. The troops are from most of the republics, so far as we can ascertain, and they are led by Japanese officers—and by a man we believed was Operator 5! He was the one who organized the invasion, working in the South American capitals and persuading the governments to join him in a war on America!"

Operator 5's cup of bitterness was full at that moment. With America divided, torn asunder, and ready to fall piecemeal into the avid hands of the Japanese, all that he had struggled for seemed hopelessly lost. Dismally he admitted that America's sun had set—until his eyes fell upon Mary Reid. Triumphant, exultant, her face wreathed in glad smiles, she was marching between her two men, happy again.

Mary Reid's sun had set, too, but now a new day had dawned for her—just as a new, glorious day must dawn for America! Defeated? In that revealing moment Operator 5 knew that he had just begun to fight! With clenched fists and hard, grimly determined eyes he strode down from that porch to face the stern battle that waited for him—and his beloved America!

AUTHOR'S NOTE: The Union severed, the States divided into three hostile camps—that desperate situation was sufficient to appall Operator 5 and the patriots who rallied round him. But even darker days were in store for America. With his ravenous grip on two-thirds of the country, the Yellow Vulture hovered over what was left of the United States and pulled from his

OPERATOR 5

Pandora's box of tricks weapons from which the civilized world shuddered. The detailed account of the epochal struggle in which Operator 5 matched wits and courage with this unscrupulous master of international intrigue will be published in the next installment.

THE SPIDER

- ❑ #1: The Spider Strikes — $13.95
- ❑ #2: The Wheel of Death — $13.95
- ❑ #3: Wings of the Black Death — $13.95
- ❑ #4: City of Flaming Shadows — $13.95
- ❑ #5: Empire of Doom! — $13.95
- ❑ #6: Citadel of Hell — $13.95
- ❑ #7: The Serpent of Destruction — $13.95
- ❑ #8: The Mad Horde — $13.95
- ❑ #9: Satan's Death Blast — $13.95
- ❑ #10: The Corpse Cargo — $13.95
- ❑ #11: Prince of the Red Looters — $13.95
- ❑ #12: Reign of the Silver Terror — $13.95
- ❑ #13: Builders of the Dark Empire — $13.95
- ❑ #14: Death's Crimson Juggernaut — $13.95
- ❑ #15: The Red Death Rain — $13.95
- ❑ #16: The City Destroyer — $13.95
- ❑ #17: The Pain Emperor — $13.95
- ❑ #18: The Flame Master — $13.95
- ❑ #19: Slaves of the Crime Master — $13.95
- ❑ #20: Reign of the Death Fiddler — $13.95
- ❑ #21: Hordes of the Red Butcher — $13.95
- ❑ #22: Dragon Lord of the Underworld — $13.95
- ❑ #23: Master of the Death-Madness — $13.95
- ❑ #24: King of the Red Killers — $13.95
- ❑ #25: Overlord of the Damned — $13.95
- ❑ #26: Death Reign of the Vampire King — $13.95
- ❑ #27: Emperor of the Yellow Death — $13.95
- ❑ #28: The Mayor of Hell — $13.95
- ❑ #29: Slaves of the Murder Syndicate — $13.95
- ❑ #30: Green Globes of Death — $13.95
- ❑ #31: The Cholera King — $13.95
- ❑ #32: Slaves of the Dragon — $13.95
- ❑ #33: Legions of Madness — $12.95
- ❑ #34: Laboratory of the Damned — $12.95
- ❑ #35: Satan's Sightless Legion — $12.95
- ❑ #36: The Coming of the Terror — $12.95
- ❑ #37: The Devil's Death-Dwarfs — $12.95
- ❑ #38: City of Dreadful Night — $12.95
- ❑ #39: Reign of the Snake Men — $12.95
- ❑ #40: Dictator of the Damned — $12.95
- ❑ #41: The Mill-Town Massacres — $12.95
- ❑ #42: Satan's Workshop — $12.95
- ❑ #43: Scourge of the Yellow Fangs — $12.95
- ❑ #44: The Devil's Pawnbroker — $12.95
- ❑ #45: Voyage of the Coffin Ship — $12.95
- ❑ #46: The Man Who Ruled in Hell — $13.95
- ❑ #47: Slaves of the Black Monarch — $13.95
- ❑ #48: Machineguns Over the White House — $13.95
- ❑ #49: The City That Dared Not Eat — $13.95
- ❑ #50: Master of the Flaming Horde — $13.95
- ❑ #51: Satan's Switchboard — $13.95
- ❑ #52: Legions of the Accursed Light — $13.95
- ❑ #53: The City of Lost Men — $13.95
- ❑ #54: The Grey Horde Creeps — $13.95
- ❑ #55: City of Whispering Death — $13.95
- ❑ #56: When Thousands Slept in Hell — $13.95
- ❑ #57: Satan's Shakles — $14.95
- ❑ #58: The Emperor From Hell — $14.95
- ❑ #59: The Devil's Candlesticks — $14.95
- ❑ #60: The City That Paid to Die — $14.95
- ❑ #61: The Spider at Bay — $14.95
- ❑ #62: Scourge of the Black Legions — $14.95
- ❑ #63: The Withering Death — $14.95
- ❑ #64: Claws of the Golden Dragon — $14.95
- ❑ #65: The Song of Death — $14.95
- ❑ #66: The Silver Death Reign — $14.95
- ❑ #67: Blight of the Blazing Eye — $14.95
- ❑ #68: King of the Fleshless Legion — $14.95
- ❑ #69: Rule of the Monster Men — $16.95
- ❑ #70: The Spider and the Slaves of Hell — $16.95
- ❑ #71: The Spider and the Fire God — $16.95
- ❑ #72: The Corpse Broker — $16.95
- ❑ #73: The Spider and the Eyeless Legion — $16.95
- ❑ #74: The Spider and the Faceless One — $16.95
- ❑ #75: Satan's Murder Machines — $16.95
- ❑ #76: The Spider and the Pain Master — $16.95
- ❑ #77: Hell's Sales Manager — $16.95
- ❑ #78: Slaves of the Laughing Death — $16.95
- ❑ #79: The Man From Hell — $16.95
- ❑ #80: The Spider and the War Emperor — $16.95
- ❑ *NEW:* #81: Judgement of the Damned — $17.95

THE WESTERN RAIDER

- ❑ #1: Guns of the Damned — $13.95
- ❑ #2: The Hawk Rides Back from Death — $13.95
- ❑ #3: Gun-Call for the Lost Legion — $13.95
- ❑ #4: The Law of Silver Trent — $13.95
- ❑ #5: The Gun-Prayer of Silver Trent — $13.95
- ❑ #6: Silver Trent Rides Alone — $13.95

CAPTAIN SATAN

- ❑ #1: The Mask of the Damned — $13.95
- ❑ #2: Parole for the Dead — $13.95
- ❑ #3: The Dead Man Express — $13.95
- ❑ #4: A Ghost Rides the Dawn — $13.95
- ❑ #5: The Ambassador From Hell — $13.95

DR. YEN SIN

- ❑ #1: Mystery of the Dragon's Shadow — $12.95
- ❑ #2: Mystery of the Golden Skull — $12.95
- ❑ #3: Mystery of the Singing Mummies — $12.95

THE MASKED MARKSMAN

- ❑ #1: Death Takes an Encore — $16.95
- ❑ #2: Death's Understudy — $16.95
- ❑ #3: Death Steals the Act — $16.95
- ❑ #4: Top Billing for Murder — $16.95